THE TABLES ARE TURNED!

"Those prisoners are Doc Savage's men!"

"Of course they're Doc Savage's gang," Hoke bellowed. "They came down here by plane three days ago!"

"But——"

"Tried to grab the treasure! We captured 'em!"

The unthinkable happens to Doc Savage and his amazing crew in

THE PIRATE'S GHOST!

Bantam Books by Kenneth Robeson
Ask your bookseller for the books you have missed

THE MAN OF BRONZE
THE THOUSAND-HEADED MAN
METEOR MENACE
THE POLAR TREASURE
BRAND OF THE WEREWOLF
THE LOST OASIS
THE MONSTERS
THE LAND OF TERROR
THE MYSTIC MULLAH
THE PHANTOM CITY
FEAR CAY
QUEST OF QUI
LAND OF ALWAYS-NIGHT
THE FANTASTIC ISLAND
MURDER MELODY
THE SPOOK LEGION
THE RED SKULL
THE SARGASSO OGRE
PIRATE OF THE PACIFIC
THE SECRET IN THE SKY
COLD DEATH
THE CZAR OF FEAR
FORTRESS OF SOLITUDE
THE GREEN EAGLE
THE DEVIL'S PLAYGROUND
DEATH IN SILVER
THE MYSTERY UNDER THE SEA
THE DEADLY DWARF
THE OTHER WORLD
THE FLAMING FALCONS
THE ANNIHILIST
THE SQUEAKING GOBLINS
MAD EYES
THE TERROR IN THE NAVY
DUST OF DEATH
RESURRECTION DAY
HEX
RED SNOW
WORLD'S FAIR GOBLIN
THE DAGGER IN THE SKY
MERCHANTS OF DISASTER
THE GOLD OGRE
THE MAN WHO SHOOK THE EARTH
THE SEA MAGICIAN
THE MEN WHO SMILED NO MORE
THE MIDAS MAN
LAND OF LONG JUJU
THE FEATHERED OCTOPUS
THE SEA ANGEL
DEVIL ON THE MOON
HAUNTED OCEAN
THE VANISHER
THE MENTAL WIZARD
HE COULD STOP THE WORLD
THE GOLDEN PERIL
THE GIGGLING GHOSTS
POISON ISLAND
THE MUNITIONS MASTER
THE YELLOW CLOUD
THE MAJII
THE LIVING FIRE MENACE
THE PIRATE'S GHOST

THE PIRATE'S GHOST

A DOC SAVAGE ADVENTURE

BY KENNETH ROBESON

A NATIONAL GENERAL COMPANY

THE PIRATE'S GHOST
*A Bantam Book / published by arrangement with
The Condé Nast Publications Inc.*

*PRINTING HISTORY
Originally published in* DOC SAVAGE *Magazine April 1938
Bantam edition published July 1971*

Published simultaneously in the United States and Canada

Bantam Books are published by Bantam Books, Inc., a National General company. Its trade-mark, consisting of the words "Bantam Books" and the portrayal of a bantam, is registered in the United States Patent Office and in other countries. Marca Registrada. Bantam Books, Inc., 666 Fifth Avenue, New York, N.Y. 10019.

PRINTED IN THE UNITED STATES OF AMERICA

CONTENTS

THE PIRATE'S GHOST

Chapter I

OLD ONE OF THE DESERT

"SAGEBRUSH" SMITH was undoubtedly not the first Smith who got into trouble without expecting it.

However, Sagebrush Smith managed to confine his troubles to the ordinary ones of a cow-puncher until the advent of a certain fifteenth day of March. This fifteenth of March followed the fourteenth, which was the day Sagebrush Smith got fired. He got canned off the Lazy Y spread for giving the round-up boss, "Hoke" McGee, what he called "a bust in the snoot" over a trifling matter of who had put a deceased rattlesnake in Sagebrush Smith's bedroll.

Sagebrush was scared of rattlesnakes, also of red-eye whisky and women. However, these three items, of all the things Sagebrush had encountered in his twenty-four years of life, were the only things he had ever been scared of. He certainly wasn't afraid of Hoke McGee.

Sagebrush Smith was a long, gangling young man with a freckled hide, and he had no cares. He was not, fortunately or unfortunately—depending on the outlook—very ambitious. There was, in fact, only one thing he really wanted to do, if he ever got around to it: he wanted to see a fellow he had read about, a man named Doc Savage. He just wanted to have a look at this Doc Savage. He had never told any one about the yen. He figured they would think it kind of silly.

Having been fired, and having offered, in a warm moment, to unravel cartridges with Hoke McGee or anybody on the Lazy Y who wanted to unravel them, Sagebrush Smith slapped his Texas saddle on his Roman-nosed pinto, thonged his warbag and slicker on the back, and rode. He rode "slick-heeled"—without spurs—for his paint bronc didn't need spurs. The cayuse was next thing to a broomtail, and plenty spirited.

Some one had said there was a job repping to be had over beyond Tule Canyon, at an outfit near Sugar Loaf Butte. Sagebrush thought he might as well see. To get there, he would have to ride down into the north arm of Death Valley, over the floor, and out again. He filled his water bag at a spring about sundown, and set out across Death Valley by dark.

In the first four hours of night riding, he shot the heads off twenty-six rattlesnakes, but only half the head off the twenty-seventh.

"Boy, howdy!" Sagebrush Smith remarked. "I'm slippin'!"

That, of course, was a modest understatement. He wasn't slipping. Except for a slight technicality, he had shot the heads off twenty-seven rattlesnakes, shooting in brilliant moonlight at targets, none larger than a silver dollar, which were moving.

Then a person or persons unknown reciprocated by shooting Sagebrush Smith's bronc through the tail.

THE tail shot was a freak. Sagebrush Smith felt at once that it was an impossible shot, reflected as much when he picked himself out of the Death Valley sand. Sagebrush was about to flop down in the sand again for caution's sake, but thought of the sidewinders and remained on his feet. He'd take his chances with bullets.

The paint pony left there as if it had a destination somewhere beyond Wyoming. The reins, Sagebrush remembered with disgust, were knotted over the jughead's neck, so he wasn't likely to stop going.

"The water bag!" exploded the cowboy.

The water bag was on the saddle! Sagebrush watched eagerly, hoping the bronc would buck the water bag off. The pinto was an enthusiastic bucker, with a style noted for getting rid of things, including, occasionally, the saddle.

But the piebald didn't buck. The horse loped over a sand dune and vanished.

When Sagebrush Smith looked around, he saw more sand dunes, plenty of them, a few heat-discouraged whiskers of mesquite, and some tall black mountains which appeared about two miles away. The mountains, he knew, were thirty miles distant. About two days of the kind of walking he would have. No one ever walked two days in Death Valley without water. He was already thirsty.

A fresh bullet arrived about that time. It cruised past somewhere overhead.

"The first one was too good," Sagebrush remarked. "And this one is too poor. There's somethin' locoed here."

He drew his six-gun and fanned two lumps of lead in the general direction of the moon. Then he listened.

Two shots answered, and the lead of the second one missed him so far that he could barely hear it sing, and the former was not much better.

"Nobody," opined Sagebrush, "could be that bum at lead-slingin'."

He had the cowboy habit of talking to himself, a failing born of the fact that for too much of his life he had been his own audience.

He banged off his gun again.

A bullet replied, and it missed him as far to the left as the others had been to the right.

"Somethin' is sure rotten in Denmark," the cowboy concluded. "Whoever is turnin' loose them blue whistlers ain't shootin' straight because it, him or her, *can't* shoot straight."

Having thus decided, he concluded it was safe to advance, and likewise very advisable. He had to get water, or the big black birds with the raw, red necks would have a man to eat.

Sagebrush advanced. He got his boots full of sand, his exposed hide covered with 'skeet scratches, and had his hair lifted assorted times by sidewinders. Twice, scorpions did their best to sock stingers through his boots into his legs, but failed because he was wearing good twenty-dollar Justins built for service.

"Damn all deserts!" he said feelingly.

Then he came upon the old man.

THE old man was wanting to shoot somebody. He had his rifle in his hand, a frantic fear and a grim desperation in his bloodshot old eyes, and awful agony working in the wrinkles of his old baboon face.

He wore scuffed old leather boots, laced khaki pants, a rag over one shoulder that had been a shirt, and he had an old body that looked as though it was made out of rake handles. He kept shooting little gouts of blood out of his mouth.

Sagebrush Smith slipped around a mesquite clump and jumped in the middle of the old man's back. When he saw the kind of thing he had jumped onto, he got off again.

He got down beside the old duffer and straightened him out on the sand and put the rifle to one side. He wet his handkerchief with water from a canteen the old man had tied to his belt and wiped off the old fellow's wasted face.

"Golly, pop, I'm sorry," he said.

The old man looked steadily at Sagebrush Smith and bubbled a little as he breathed.

"I was afraid you wouldn't make it, Doc's man," he said. "I kept hearing them shooting at you. Just one shot at a time. The shots kept getting closer. I knew they were trying to pick you off before you made it."

Sagebrush Smith, who was as shaggy as a young jackass on the outside, and about as handsome, had a likeable, kindly nature; and he wanted to humor an old man who was half mad and dying in the desert.

"I fixed 'em," he said.

The old man of the desert looked Sagebrush Smith's long, gangling young frame up and down.

"Doc's man," he said, "I'm glad to see you."

Being called "Doc's man" had Sagebrush Smith puzzled. He finally figured it out and decided that the old fellow thought he had come from the doctor.

"Buck up, old-timer," he said. "Stick out your horns and show some sand. You gotta last until I can take you to the doctor."

"You came to take me to Doc?"

"Yeah. Betcher boots."

"Won't do no good," the old man said. "I've got cancer. I've had it two years, and I haven't got any insides left to speak of."

SAGEBRUSH SMITH got up on his feet rather quickly, because he couldn't have stayed there on his knees without feeling sick. He stamped his boots in the powder-fine sand and jammed his hands in his pockets, then took them out again and peered around for something to get his mind off the dying old man. Mentally, he added a fourth item to the list of things he was scared of: a man dying slowly.

So, in trying to get away from a sight that turned his stomach, Sagebrush Smith walked around—came upon the amazing laboratory. First, he only saw an old adobe hut, and thought: "This is a funny place for one of them things." Then he looked inside and saw that it was really something unusual.

The mud walls had been plastered inside, and the plaster painted white. Around three walls of the room ran a bench, with shelves above and bins below; and the shelves and bins were crowded with neat arrays of copper wire, silver wire, copper rods and silver rods, coils, bakelite insulating panels, bottles, boxes, jars, and innumerable things that resembled radio vacuum tubes, and yet weren't quite like vacuum tubes.

It was very cool in the hut, leading Sagebrush Smith to realize the interior was air-conditioned, exactly like the movie house in Goldfield. He was a little surprised.

He was more surprised as he went along. The box in the center of the room intrigued him. A skylight let moonglow in through the roof and he could see the box. It was about as tall as himself—around six feet—and about a dozen feet long by eight feet wide.

"Creepin' Moses!" said Sagebrush Smith. "It's solid silver!"

It wasn't. His imagination had run away with him. It was lead, he decided, after he gave it a good scratching with the point of his pocketknife.

One whisker of shiny copper tubing stuck up out of the top of the lead box.

After he had moseyed around the thing a while, Sagebrush found a door, and being of an inquiring disposition, he opened the door and went in, after first striking a match.

He looked around the inside of the lead box. He saw a lot of stuff that he didn't understand. In fact, he saw practically nothing that he did understand, and he began to wish he wasn't so ignorant about electricity.

Sagebrush rubbed his jaw and scratched his head and began touching things, but an electric spark jumped out and bit him, and he stopped that.

There was a small box on the floor which aroused Sagebrush's curiosity. He polished the lock on the box thoughtfully with the ball of a thumb. He could see it was the kind of lock you couldn't pick. The box itself was of high-quality steel. Sagebrush tried his jackknife on it, and the metal of the box turned the razor edge of the knife blade, and didn't even scratch. He lifted the box to test its weight, and grunted with the effort.

"Almost as heavy as Hoke McGee's opinion of himself," he remarked.

He went back outside.

"Your layout's got me guessin', pop," he said.

THE old man was propped up on his hands, straining, hurting himself listening to the whispering night sounds of the desert sands. He turned his head, and there was a wild look on his face.

"I think I heard some of them creeping!" he croaked. "Creeping over the sand!"

Sagebrush Smith put the palm of a hand on the nape of his neck, just to reassure himself that the short hairs were not standing on end.

"That's just sidewinders, old-timer," he said.

There was a silence filled with the kind of stillness that only comes in Death Valley—stillness of utter death and time abysmal. Then a breeze, a small lost breeze, came feeling over the dunes, seeking in the mesquite, sifting in the sands, and sighing.

Sagebrush Smith took off his hat, mopped his forehead and grinned foolishly. He felt the need of doing something to break the spell, so he kicked out, like a boy, with one foot. His toe hit a rock.

He peered at the rock, then got down on his knees, brushed sand away and kept on brushing until he had a space cleared the size of a bunk house table. The rock bore grotesque carvings and silly-looking hen-track marks.

Sagebrush Smith got to his feet, kicked around in the sand and uncovered other such rocks. Then it dawned on him that the stones lay all around; some of the huge ones were even the reason for the sand dunes being here.

"We're in one of them mysterious ruined cities or my name ain't Sagebrush," he muttered.

The old man said, "That was in my letter to Doc," very weakly.

"Some fellers that called themselves archæologists were in Death Valley one time," Sagebrush continued. "They figured there had been cities in here thousands of years ago, but they couldn't figure out much else about them."*

"That is why I came here," the old man said.

"Oh," Sagebrush Smith said.

The dying man closed his eyes for a while and rested. After a moment or two he started talking again.

"Did Doc remember me?" he asked suddenly. "Did Doc remember old Meander Surett?"

"Yeah," said Sagebrush. " 'Course he remembered you."

Old Meander Surett closed his eyes. He appeared about as pleased as he could be.

"I'm not suprised that he remembered," he said. "I was one of the world's greatest authorities on electrical research —before I disappeared."

---

* These prehistoric ruins, some actually stretching for miles on the heat-seared floor of Death Valley in California, are something of a puzzle to archæologists.

KENNETH ROBESON

Chapter II

THE MAN-CAPTIVE

THE desert night was either very still, or it was made weird by the tiny whirls of wind that went scurrying through the sand dunes, although some of the winds weren't so tiny and traveled like Kansas whirlwinds, picking up fine sand, lifting it two and three hundred feet, looking in the moonlight like cinnamon-robed giants hobble-skirting along.

Sagebrush Smith hunkered on his high-heeled boots and felt funny. Not humorous. Just funny. The old man, Meander Surett, was dying, and Sagebrush had started out by agreeing with everything, hoping that would soothe the old fellow. Now he began to see that he was walking into something. Meander Surett apparently had expected some one named Doc to arrive. He thought Sagebrush Smith was one of this Doc's representatives.

Curiosity assailed Sagebrush. He wanted to know who Doc was. He wanted to know the purpose of all that stuff in the adobe hut. He wondered what was in the alloy-steel locked box. He would like to know why the place was located in one of the prehistoric ruins on the floor of Death Valley.

He could not ask any of these questions without exciting Meander Surett and speeding his death.

"Sagebrush," said Meander Surett unexpectedly.

"Yeah?"

"How did *they* find out you were coming?"

"They? Who do you mean?"

"The men who followed you."

"Oh." Sagebrush Smith hunted in his mind for a lie. "I don't know. I thought maybe you could tell me."

"They've been spying on me for years," the dying man said weakly. "I have been working here for ten years. It was about three years ago that I first noticed them spying. I guess they knew I sent Doc a message."

"Message?"

"Yes. The letter. Doc got it, of course, or he wouldn't have sent you."

Sagebrush Smith swallowed. "Oh, sure," he said.

"I don't know the men who watched me," croaked Meander Surett.

"You'd better be quiet," the cowboy urged.

Meander Surett coughed and bubbled. "Get me the metal box in the lead-insulated experimental chamber."

SAGEBRUSH SMITH got the box. It was heavy enough that he was sweating and out of breath by the time he had it at the side of Meander Surett.

"Now," Meander Surett gurgled, "unbuckle my money belt."

The money belt was made of chamois. It was fat and heavy, and Sagebrush Smith, when he was ordered to do so, looked inside.

"Geewhilikers!" he said.

"There is about seven thousand dollars' worth of gold dust left," Meander Surett said. "I had half a million dollars when I started experimenting ten years ago. I had the money changed into gold dust because nobody is suspicious of an old man who comes out of the desert with a little gold dust. They think he is a prospector."

Sagebrush Smith was stunned. "You mean," he muttered, "that you spent half a million here in the desert?"

"It was worth it." The dying man reached out a wasted hand to the shiny metal box. "*This*"—he patted the box—"is going to change the course of all mankind!"

Sagebrush Smith wiped his forehead. "Uh-huh," he muttered. He didn't know what to think.

"Use as much of the seven thousand as you need for expenses," said Meander Surett.

"Expenses?"

"Plane fare, hotels, taxicabs and so on." The old man had a coughing spell. "You can give the rest to Sally."

"Sally?"

"My daughter. Sally Surett." Old Meander Surett smiled in spite of pain and weakness. "She may call herself Nola. She never did like the name Sally. Her full name is Sally Nola Surett. She lives at 110 North Boulevard, in New York City. You better write that down."

Sagebrush Smith swallowed.

"I'll remember it," he said. "Sally Nola Surett at 110 North Boulevard, New York."

"Take her to Doc," ordered Meander Surett, "and give the box to her and to Doc, to be owned and shared jointly." He shut his eyes and shuddered. "The contents must be used to benefit mankind, not—the other."

"To Doc—who?" Sagebrush Smith asked involuntarily.

"Why, to Doc Savage," Meander Surett said.

"Doc Savage!" Sagebrush Smith took off his hat. "Blazes!"

THERE is probably no institution of mankind better equipped with reading matter than the cowboy bunk house. The height of the stack of magazines in the corner will vary with the seasons, shrinking in the winter when they are handy for starting fires, but usually it ranges around shoulder high. So Sagebrush Smith had read about Doc Savage.

He had read of Doc Savage several times. Once in a medical journal, twice in a physical culture magazine, and a number of times in magazines devoted to science and mechanics. Sagebrush Smith did not believe all he read. He did not think there was any such fellow as remarkable as the Doc Savage mentioned in these magazines.

What got his dander up was a magazine stating that this Doc Savage could take a six-shooter and hit fifty silver dimes, thrown into the air, with fifty shots.

Sagebrush Smith was willing to stand on a stack of Bibles and say it couldn't be done. He knew. He'd just like to pay a visit to Doc Savage and show the fellow up.

"You want me to take this box to Doc Savage?" said Sagebrush. "And you're furnishing the expense money?"

"Yes," said old Meander Surett. "You must promise to go to Doc and my daughter, Sally."

Sagebrush Smith suddenly became enthusiastic about the job.

"You're on, old-timer," he said earnestly. "But what's in the box?"

The old man was apparently too far gone to hear.

"What's in the box?" the cowboy asked more loudly.

The dying old man rolled his head. His eyes were strange.

"There is a sheaf of data in the box," he mumbled. "That will explain everything."

"But where's the key to the box?"

"It has already been mailed to Doc Savage," old Meander Surett mumbled.

"Oh," said Sagebrush Smith.

Old Meander Surett's throat began to rattle. Sagebrush Smith had heard that throats rattle when people die.

"Take it easy, pop!" Sagebrush mumbled.

The old man's hands fastened to the cowboy's arm like claws.

"Son, they'll try to take it from you!" he croaked.

"They won't have much luck," Sagebrush said soothingly. "Don't rile yourself, old-timer."

The old man made noises. The bite of his fingers tightened.

"Son," he gulped, "I haven't told you everything!"

"No?" Sagebrush said curiously.

"I caught two of them—one of the men watching me." Meander Surett was shaking. "I killed one of them. I took the other captive. I've got him now—a prisoner. Tried—to make him—talk—for months."

His words were beginning to be separated by the rattling.

"Sure, you killed one and you've got the other prisoner," Sagebrush said. "Take it easy, pop."

"The—prisoner—over there!" Old Meander Surett croaked.

"Eh?"

The dying man pointed. "Over—there! Chained!"

"You mean you've got a man *chained* over there?" the cowboy demanded incredulously.

"Fastened—with—a—a chain. He wouldn't—talk——"

The old man's eyes rolled and he could only make noises.

SAGEBRUSH SMITH got to his feet, took a step or two in the direction in which Meander Surett had pointed. He stared. He bent over to see better.

The mesquite was tall and thick and cast black shadows. It was too dark to make out anything much. The cowboy licked his lips, then advanced.

Suddenly, Sagebrush jerked to a stop and snatched at his six-gun. He had heard a noise, a small, whimpering sound. He listened. His pulse was a-booming. Then there was a small movement. *Something was really there!*

Holding his gun in one hand, he advanced. It was very dark. His foot struck something, and feeling with his free hand, he found a chain. He tugged the chain. It jerked in his hand, and the low whimpering came again.

"Hey, feller!" Sagebrush Smith called softly. "How long has the old man had you a prisoner here?"

The whimper was his only answer.

Sagebrush Smith struck a match.

There was only a mangy and half-starved coyote pup on the end of the chain. And around about was bedding and odds and ends of clothing and enough of the kind of food that a man eats to show that old Meander Surett had been treating the coyote as a man.

Meander Surett was dead when Sagebrush Smith went back to him.

Chapter III

HOKE McGEE

WHEN Sagebrush Smith guided two donkeys up to the Lazy Y ranch house, he was not doing it because he wanted to, but because he had to have water. There had not been enough in Meander Surett's canteen. The Lazy Y had the only water on the route to the nearest railroad town.

The two donkeys had obviously belonged to old Meander Surett, for Sagebrush had found them hobbled in the Death Valley sand dunes after he buried the scientist and freed the half-starved coyote. He'd appropriated one donkey to carry the box, and one to carry himself, although the last hadn't worked out; after trying to ride for twenty miles, a habit of both mountain canaries of trying unexpectedly to take a bite out of his leg had led him to favor walking.

Hoke McGee, the Lazy Y foreman, looked on the advent of Sagebrush Smith with no favor at all.

"I thought we run you away from here once," he growled.

"Nobody ever run me away from anywhere," said Sagebrush.

He grabbed a donkey by an ear with one hand and held the animal while he unlashed the metal box with the other hand.

"Take your brothers"—Hoke McGee pointed at the donkeys—"and get the hell out of here!"

"Maybe you'd like to make me?" suggested Sagebrush.

Hoke McGee scowled.

"Maybe," Sagebrush said, "you and your whole danged Lazy Y outfit would like to try to make me go?"

Hoke McGee was a perfectly safe fellow to quarrel with—as long as you were looking at him. It was after dark, or when he was behind you, that he was dangerous. This was a fact that Sagebrush well knew.

Hoke McGee was not of the true west, not of cactus and purple sage. He was a product of crooked carnivals and low gypping. An old carney man of the never-give-the-sucker-a-break school. When the carney shell games went out, he took up cow-punching on the Lazy Y, the owner of which was a distant relative, as well as a bird of similar feather. They called him "Hoke" because he liked to brag about the hokum the yaps used to fall for.

Hoke McGee wasn't yellow, but he was cautious enough not to hit out when there was a chance of getting hit back. He thought himself quite a smoothie. Physically, he was short and broad and ran more to body and arms than to legs or head.

Sagebrush Smith always said that if you could find a he-toad five feet five inches tall and take the warts off him, you would have Hoke McGee.

"I'm stayin' for supper," announced Sagebrush Smith.

"The hell you are!" snarled Hoke McGee.

"The hell I ain't!" said Sagebrush.

Having unlashed the metal box, Sagebrush Smith got under it with both arms, and kneed the donkey in the ribs to make the animal jump out from under the case. Sagebrush staggered over to the shade of the bunk house and put the box down.

"What's that?" Hoke McGee demanded.

"That," said Sagebrush Smith, "is a gookus-wookus."

"A what?"

"Somethin' to make fools ask questions."

Ten minutes later, the owner of the Lazy Y appeared, in tow of Hoke McGee.

"You'll have to pay for your supper," the owner said shortly.

"You're dang tootin' I'll pay for it!" declared Sagebrush Smith. "I'm particular who I take favors from."

"It'll cost you five dollars," said the owner of the Lazy Y.

"It'll cost me two bits," corrected Sagebrush, "which is more than the kind of chow you serve here is worth."

And because he wanted to devil them, he whipped out his money belt and made them weigh out a gold nugget and give him change for twenty-five cents. He knew nothing would hurt them like letting them see that he had a nice gold dust stake. He figured he had them bluffed to a point where they wouldn't dare do anything about it.

That was a mistake.

HOKE MCGEE and the owner did not eat in the bunk house with the rest of the rannys. They ate in the ranch house and had better food. To-night they had a conference.

"How much money did Smith have when he left here?" asked Hoke McGee.

"Not much more than forty dollars," said the owner of the Lazy Y.

"Now he's got a belt full of gold. Between six and eight thousand dollars' worth."

"What's in that box?" asked the owner.

"I don't know," said Hoke McGee, "but I bet you it's full of gold."

"Why?"

"I tried to lift it. The thing weighs anyway two hundred pounds."

"Gold, eh?"

"Why, hell, it couldn't be anythin' else, boss. This ranny goes off in the desert empty-handed and comes back with a belt of gold, an iron box and two donkeys. Now me and you both know that he either got the stuff by robbin' somebody, or he found somebody that had died in the desert. And either way it stands to reason there's gold in the box."

"Hm-m. That's too bad," said the owner.

Hoke McGee grinned evilly.

"We'll know just how bad it is," he said, "by along about mornin'."

Sagebrush Smith was fully aware that the Lazy Y would

have its cupidity aroused by the gold dust and the box. But Sagebrush was reckless enough and salty enough that he didn't give, as he put it, "a tinker's damn!"

However, after supper, and immediately prior to sunset, he put on a little demonstration for effect. He had received seven silver dimes as change for his supper payment of gold dust, and he took the seven dimes outside, and four poker chips. He tossed up the seven dimes, one at a time, and hit two out of the seven with bullets from his six-gun, firing, however, twelve times.

"That goes to show," Sagebrush declared, "that it can't be done. *Nobody can do that trick!*"

Then he threw the four poker chips into the air and shot them into a myriad of pieces with four bullets from his six-shooter.

"Of course," he announced, "that last ain't no trick at all."

Sagebrush blew the smoke out of his hogleg, gave it a spectacular twirl on his fingers, and smacked it into the leather. He figured he had cooled off any ambitions anybody might have had toward the box. He was rather pleased with himself.

His bubble of pleasure got a pin stuck in it when he went back to the metal box.

A man was crouched over the box, who held a scrap of paper in one hand. With the other hand, the man was trying to pick the lock with a wire. He was intent on the business.

Sagebrush walked up to the man and drew back and gave the fellow an enthusiastic kick. Various things then happened, none of them expected.

THE crouching man squawked, sailed completely over the box, turned in the air and landed facing Sagebrush Smith.

Sagebrush then got a look at the man and had the impression that he had kicked a bull baboon.

The paper the man had been holding fluttered away into the sagebrush.

The baboon of a man sailed back over the box and hit Sagebrush Smith. Hit him, to the salty cowhand's everlasting mortification, before Sagebrush could draw his six-shooter.

The punch combined electricity and dynamite. Sagebrush saw strange lights, suspected he was swapping ends in the air, and found himself flat on the ground.

Sagebrush unleathered his six-gun and threw lead. His first bullet went into the sand, the second went toward the moon, and he wasn't sure about the next two. However, they must have come close to the apish man, because the latter turned and sought safety. He reached the tall sage and vanished by the simple expedient of bending double.

His head had cleared, so Sagebrush bounded up and charged after the stranger. The fellow had been at least a foot and a half shorter than Sagebrush, and the latter resented being knocked on his ear by such a sawed-off specimen.

However, for a man whose legs appeared to be a good deal shorter than his arms, the stranger made remarkable time.

Sagebrush did not get another glimpse of him.

The Lazy Y rannys and their husky foreman, Hoke McGee, had arrived by that time, looking puzzled and demanding to know what had happened.

"I just met," Sagebrush explained, "a spook with hair on his chest." He felt of his jaw and grimaced. "The homeliest dang jigger I ever seen!"

Following which he made pointed inquiries about whether or not the Lazy Y had hired any new hands during his absence, and because he was so plainly in an irritated mood, he got civil answers. Sagebrush became convinced that the short, apish marauder was as much a stranger to the Lazy Y men as to himself.

"Wait a minute!" Hoke exclaimed. "Two strange dudes sifted through here the day after you left. One of 'em was a feller built with kind of a thin waist like a mud-dauber and dressed fancy as Mrs. Astor's horse. Hell, he even carried a cane!"

"This galoot that erupted on me didn't look nothin' like that," Sagebrush grunted.

"Yeah, but there was an hombre with this fashion plate," said Hoke McGee, "that was dang nigh as wide as he was tall, had rusty-lookin' hair over 'im, and a face that was somethin' to stop a clock. After he left, one of the rannys looked in the dictionary under orang-outang and found somethin' that looked like 'im."

"That's my honeybunch!" said Sagebrush.

A Lazy Y cowboy chuckled. "Don't forget," he said, "the pig and the monkey them two fellers had along."

"The *what?*" said Sagebrush.

"They had two pets," said the cowboy. "A pig and a monkey. Anyhow, I guess it was a monkey. There was some argument about that."

Sagebrush Smith rubbed his jaw again. "This is sure a funny world."

"Those two men," said Hoke McGee, "were lookin' for some gent named Meander Surett."

Sagebrush stopped rubbing his jaw. "Huh?"

"Meander Surett, they called him."

"Why, dang it, that's the old geezer who gave me the box and gold——" Sagebrush swallowed. He hadn't intended to say even that much.

He would have done much better to have gone ahead with explanations, because Hoke McGee had made a serious error. Hoke had misunderstood the fragment of a sentence. He thought Sagebrush had said *"box of gold."*

SAGEBRUSH SMITH did some cogitating, after which he got himself a good-sized club and went looking for his donkeys. He had discovered that the jackasses would stand and let him catch them if he carried a club, but would run like rabbits if he was empty-handed.

Having captured one of the donkeys, the cowboy lashed his box to the back of the animal. This was work, but he didn't want to leave the box lying around, even for a few minutes; not even while he rode out to have a look at his back trail before it got dark.

Sagebrush's examination of his back trail showed him that two men, two burros, one pig and one monkey had tracked him out of the desert to the Lazy Y ranch. The two men were evidently better at hiding footprints than he was at following them, because he failed to find them before night fell.

Somewhat puzzled, Sagebrush went back toward the Lazy Y ranch house. Two men had followed him out of the desert. Not the slightest doubt of that. He frowned. He never had been quite able to convince himself that old Meander Surett had been insane. Of course, the poor old man had been mentally unbalanced during the last weeks of his life, but as for prior to that, there was a question in Sagebrush's mind. And thinking of the dying old man's wild and repeated insistence that there *had* been some one watching him. . . . Sagebrush got out his gun and gave it a grim examination.

"I'm gonna do some ventilatin' the next time I see either of them jaspers!" he declared.

Reaching the Lazy Y ranch house, Sagebrush unloaded the chest, and it was while doing this that something came back to him. He snapped his fingers gravely.

"Dang!" he said. "I forgot all about that paper!"

He borrowed a flashlight from the scowling Lazy Y foreman, went to the spot where he had caught the mysterious, apish gentleman examining the box, and searched industriously for half an hour before he found what he wanted—the sheet of paper the apish fellow had dropped. Considering that it was obviously only part of a communication, it was interesting:

> —theories undoubtedly substantiated, the belief being held by others besides Thomas A. Edison. The Edison experiments were unfortunately begun late in that great man's career, and were interrupted by the gifted inventor's death. I mention this because the work of these scientists was the starting point for my own.
>
> The contents of the metal case cannot be considered of anything less than world-shaking importance.
>
> The case is of vault steel, the type which is impervious to cutting torches. It is a foot and a half deep, two feet wide and three feet one inch in length. The lock is the best obtainable.

There had originally been much more to the communication, apparently, but it ended there. This segment had been torn from the rest, top and bottom, evidently by using a ruler as a straight edge.

SAGEBRUSH folded the paper, stowed it in a pocket and went to contemplate the box. He was having an attack of intense curiosity about the contents, but unless he was mistaken, the metal case would be harder to crack than a safe.

He was sitting on the box dragging at a cigarette when hoofbeats rattled up to the Lazy Y corral. Sagebrush shifted so that his gun was handier. He needn't have bothered. It was only the Lazy Y wrangatang, who had ridden to town for the mail.

The mail included the usual bundle of newspapers.

Sagebrush Smith dragged the metal box into the bunk house where he could watch it; then he picked up a newspaper idly. His casualness didn't last long.

PROFESSOR MEANDER SURETT DIES
ONE OF WORLD'S GREAT
SCIENTISTS

Body Buried Near Death Valley Laboratory
Believed He Worked Alone There
Vanished Years Ago

"Great Muley steers!" said Sagebrush Smith.

He read the two columns on the first page down to where it said "Turn to Page Two," then discovered that page two was all about Meander Surett. The pictures were of the man Sagebrush had found in the desert, or rather, of the man as he would have been ten years ago in good health.

The story said Meander Surett pioneered wireless; ranked almost with Marconi. Meander Surett formulated the most acceptable theory of cosmic rays. Meander Surett pioneered ultra-short-wave radio.

There was almost everything about Meander Surett except what Sagebrush Smith wanted to know. And that was: Who had found the body? Sagebrush Smith had buried the old scientist three days ago, and he had not yet told any one anything. Who, then, had found out the old fellow was dead? And how had they gotten the news to the papers? There weren't any telephones nearer to Death Valley than the one which ran from town to the Lazy Y.

"Ah, frog feathers!" complained Sagebrush Smith.

It got dark at eight o'clock. About nine the telephone in the ranch house rang and the operator said, "New York is calling Mr. Hoke McGee."

"This is Hoke," said Hoke McGee, who had happened to answer. "Uh—New York, you say? Who's callin' me from New York?"

"Mr. Barr," said the operator. "Just a moment."

Hoke McGee wrinkled what forehead he had. Barr—Barr. The only Barr he knew was Everett Everett Barr, the lawyer. Hoke McGee and Everett Everett Barr had run a carnival skin game in partnership, but that had been many years ago. Everett Everett had gone a long way since those days. He was an eminent New York attorney, he had written in his last letter, when he had turned down Hoke McGee's invitation to buy a gold mine which Hoke had all nicely salted and waiting.

"Hello, Hoke. How are you?"

It was Everett Everett, all right.

"I'm all right," said Hoke, "but if you're after that gold mine, the price has gone up."

Everett Everett Barr laughed. Mr. Barr had the heartiest and most convincing laugh of any man Hoke McGee had ever heard.

"Hoke, old pal, old boy, old friend"—Mr. Barr was always very effusive—"this is about something big. Something a lot better than any gold mine. It's really gigantic. Colossal. It's actually—well, have you read the newspapers?"

"Yeah," said Hoke wonderingly.

"Then," said Everett Everett Barr, "you know all about the great scientist, Meander Surett, who was found dead in the desert near your ranch?"

"All I know is what I read." Hoke McGee was puzzled.

"Hoke, old pard, old mate, old chunk-off-the-log, you've got to move fast. Grab your airplane, your horse, your jackass or whatever you use for transportation out there and buzz over to where they found the old scientist. You'll have to really step on it, because you've got to get there before they take the box away."

"Box?" said Hoke McGee dumbly.

"Sure. Box. Made of steel. About three feet long, two feet wide, and a foot high. Locked."

"I don't get this," Hoke complained.

"Hoke, old buddy, old sweetie, you've got to get this box for me. Get it at any cost. Any cost, see? Borrow, bribe, shoot, steal or say please! But get the box for me!"

The gist of this sank into Hoke McGee's head and he leered lovingly at the telephone.

"How much in it for me?" he asked.

"Twenty-five thousand of Uncle Sam's dollars," said Everett Everett Barr.

"Uh—wuh!" Hoke McGee swallowed twice with difficulty. *"Uh—*twenty—*what did you say?"*

"Twenty-five thousand dollars when the box is in my hands, Hoke, old son, old socks, old——"

"One box," Hoke interrupted, "coming up!"

He hung up and got out his handkerchief and removed the wetness from his forehead. Then he played leapfrog over a chair and threw down his hat and jumped on it.

"You know what?" he asked the Lazy Y owner excitedly.

"What?"

"Old Double-Everetts wants to pay us twenty-five thousand smackeroos for that box Sagebrush Smith is totin' around!"

"What? Huh? Great spades! That's just like finding twenty-five thousand!"

"Twenty-five thousand—hell! It's just like findin' a million!"

"How come?"

"Anythin' that old Double-Everetts would offer twenty-five grand for is worth a million at least. I know my Everetts!"

Chapter IV

BIG APE AND PIG MAN

WHEN Hoke McGee issued a cordial invitation to sleep in the bunk house with the boys, Sagebrush Smith bull-headedly insisted on sleeping in the ranch house with the powers that were. He figured that if Hoke wanted him in the bunk house that night, the bunk house was no place to be; but what he didn't stop to figure was that Hoke McGee knew him like a book by this time; knew that if Sagebrush was invited to sleep in the bunk house, he would insist on the ranch house instead.

So Sagebrush entered in the ranch house front bedroom, rolled back the bedcovers and looked for rattlesnakes as a matter of habit, then removed his boots and pants and got in bed. All good cowboys sleep in their shirts and underwear.

Sagebrush lay for a while and had vague sensations. He was beginning to feel something like a professional mouse-catcher who had come upon a lion. It was possible that he had taken a bite out of something huge and mysterious. Just what was in that box, anyway? He went to sleep in a bad humor, because he resented things he did not understand.

It was about three o'clock in the morning when the rat trap went off. When he heard the rat trap snap, he reared up in bed, clawed for his six-gun and pointed it at the box. He had set the rat trap and placed the box on it before he retired, so that the trap would go off if the box was lifted.

To Sagebrush's astonishment, he could not see any one near the box. And there was moonlight in the room.

To his greater astonishment, a gun snout was jammed into his right ear. He knew it was the nose of a gun because the sight cut him.

"Drop that hogleg!" gritted Hoke McGee's voice.

Sagebrush thought about what a bullet going in his right ear might do to his brains, and let fall his six-gun.

"Polecats!" he said.

Hoke McGee came around from behind the bed, much pleased with himself.

"We was all rigged for you, smart puss," he chuckled. "We had the screws loose in the window lock and the window slide greased, and we had a hole poked in the wall so we could watch you from the other room. We saw you fix the rat trap. Sit still, you!"

Hoke unlocked the door, and the Lazy Y owner came in carrying a sawed-off shotgun.

"You tote the box," Hoke told him.

The owner strained with the box, then complained, "Danged if it ain't heavy!"

Sagebrush said, "I'll skin you ginks alive!"

"Shut up!" said Hoke. "Get movin'!"

SAGEBRUSH SMITH got out of bed and walked toward the front door, feeling—with his hands held open by his ears and in his shirt tails—very much like one of the donkeys.

"Hey," he muttered. "Lemme put on my boots!"

"Heh, heh!" said Hoke viciously.

Sagebrush began to feel as though he had waded into a spring of cold water.

"You gonna take me into the desert and turn me loose without any shoes?" he gritted.

"I wouldn't be surprised," Hoke McGee said.

Sagebrush swallowed with discomfort. In the desert without shoes! Sun and weather had done something to the desert rock around Death Valley and it had become like broken glass——

Suddenly deciding he would take chances with guns

instead of the desert, Sagebrush stepped through the front door—and pitched to one side.

It was ink dark on the porch. He hit some one. Whoever he bumped into fell down.

"Blast your hide!" said the one who had fallen. He spoke in a voice remarkably like that of a child.

Sagebrush popped his eyes at what was now happening in the doorway. A rather slender man had appeared in the lighted door. This man was lean, of average height. He wore fine cordovan gentleman's riding boots, well-tailored whipcord breeches, a checked sports coat, ascot tie, pearl-gray derby with a small, bright feather in the band. He carried a slender black cane.

This male fashion-plate jerked the cane apart at the handle; it became a sword with a lean, flashing blade. The dapper man was a wizard with the sword. The point licked out and perforated Hoke McGee's gun hand and Hoke bawled and dropped his gun.

The Lazy Y owner was carrying the box. He tried to put it down, tripped and fell, landing with the box atop him. He howled as the sword cane dived like a spark and left a red line across his cheek.

Next both Hoke McGee and the Lazy Y owner made loud, sighing noises as though very sleepy, and fell on their faces and made no more moves, except to breathe. They did continue breathing.

All this happened while Sagebrush was getting to his feet. The cowboy peered to see whom he had bumped into. Suspicions were correct; it was the apish individual he had kicked earlier in the night.

"The hairy spook again!" Sagebrush grunted.

Then the Lazy Y rannys arrived.

LAZY Y cowhands had a bad reputation. They were gun-toters, and more than one had ridden the "owl hoot" trail; had rustled cattle or engaged in other thievery. No one could say they were afraid of a fight where money was involved.

Hoke McGee must have told them there was money mixed up in this, because they came storming on to the porch with lanterns, rifles and revolvers. They came boiling, fighting.

Sagebrush grabbed a man around the neck with one

hand, punched him with the other hand. He did very well. But some one stepped up and cracked him with a rifle butt and drove him against the ranch house wall so hard that he bounced. Next, he was down and high-heeled boots were walking on him.

The apish man and the dapper man were hemmed in. Backs to the ranch house wall, they fought. Some one threw a rifle; it caved in the well-dressed man's pearl-gray derby and did enough to his skull so that he kneeled down. Men landed on him. The apish man bawled, tried to rescue the other. He, too, went down.

Lazy Y hands piled on. A gun or two went off, but fighting was too close and it was too dark for effective lead-throwing. Then the fight was over suddenly and the Lazy Y had won with numbers.

"Get a rope," someone said. "We'll tie 'em up."

"I'll get it," a cowboy muttered.

He stepped off the porch, stopped.

"Who—who—who"—he pointed—"who's that?"

Sagebrush Smith, struck by the strangeness in the cowboy's voice, raised his head and looked. He saw the bronze man. It was the first time he had seen the bronze man. And he never forgot it.

The bronze man came out of the tall sagebrush and at first, walking out there in the moonlight, he seemed of average size. Then he came closer. He wasn't average size. Wasn't average anything. He seemed to grow, develop. He became a giant so perfectly proportioned that it was only when he was near other men with whom he could be compared that his tremendous stature was evident.

Sagebrush stared. It wasn't only the bronze man's size that gripped him. There was more; eyes. Even in the moonlight the man's eyes—like pools of flake gold—seemed to have a hypnotic compelling power. The man wore no hat and his hair fitted like a metallic skullcap, and was a bronze hue only slightly darker than his skin. When he moved his head tendons barred out in his neck; he walked with eerie lightness. And probably more than anything else, his calmness was impressive. He seemed entirely unconcerned.

He reached the porch and spoke. His voice was deep, cultured, remarkably toned, and had also a subtle, compelling power that was in keeping with the power of the man himself.

"Here is something," he said, "that might be interesting."

He held out a palm; an object that might have been a glass marble rolled off it, hit the porch floor with a faint, crunching sound, and became a wet spot. A wet spot for but an instant; then the wetness was gone and there was only the thin glistening of a broken, globular, glass container.

Sagebrush Smith was suddenly seized by the apish man. The fellow clutched Sagebrush's mouth and throat and shut off air from his lungs. Fighting to free himself, Sagebrush realized the other man was holding his breath, too.

Then a Lazy Y cowhand took in a deep breath and let it out in a sigh and got down on his knees. Ludicrously, the cowhand peered at the porch floor as though hunting a soft place; then he laid down. The other Lazy Y men did the same thing in quick succession until there was no one but the strange bronze man left standing.

Fully thirty additional seconds passed during which Sagebrush was not allowed to get air. He knew his face was purple. But his struggles against the apish man were absolutely futile.

Then the bronze man spoke—he, too, had held his breath.

"The anæsthetic gas has dissipated by now," he said.

THE apish man and the well-dressed man—the latter wasn't so well-dressed now—got to their feet. Both gulped air in the fashion of men who had been holding their breath.

"I thought you was in the plane headed for Meander Surett's laboratory," the apish man said sheepishly.

"I was afraid you might have a little trouble here, Monk," the bronze man explained.

The bronze man went to the vault-steel box, and picked it up—picked it up, actually, with one hand—and swung it onto a shoulder without as much as seeming to strain. Sagebrush Smith's eyes popped; he knew the weight of that box.

"Let's go," the bronze man said. "There are more men at the bunk house."

They left the ranch house, the bronze man carrying the metal case easily.

Several Lazy Y cowboys still at the bunk house—they had been delayed, probably, by the necessity for digging their weapons out of bedrolls or war-sacks—began shooting. Bullets ate off pieces of sagebrush around the retreating men.

"Your machine-pistol, Monk," the bronze giant said.

The apish man produced a weapon which slightly resembled an overgrown automatic pistol. It had a drum magazine.

"It's loaded with them new bomb bullets," "Monk" explained. "That's the reason I didn't use it."

The bronze man took the gun; pointed it in the direction of the Lazy Y buildings and pulled the trigger. Sagebrush Smith's ears were assailed by such a roar as he'd never heard before. If there could be a bull as big as Pikes Peak, and if the bull were to bawl, the noise would be about like the one the little gun made.

An entire corner of the Lazy Y ranch house flew into the air; the windmill jumped up and fell over; and part of the corral disintegrated into flying rails. Wagonloads of earth sprang into the air at points closer and closer to the bunk house. The Lazy Y rannys around the bunk house turned and fled like prairie dogs in a thunderstorm.

"That kinda discouraged 'em," Monk said.

Sagebrush Smith and his companions trotted half a mile over the arid hills into a deep dry-wash and approached two burros which were tied.

By then, Sagebrush Smith had recovered enough from general astonishment to gulp a question. *"What the heck kinda guys are you, anyhow?"* he demanded.

No one responded.

The bronze giant lowered the metal case to the sand. He showed no effects of having packed such a heavy burden at a trot for half a mile. Producing a flashlight which apparently operated from a spring-generator instead of a battery, and which emitted a thin, very white rod of light, he examined the box.

In the midst of the bronze man's scrutiny, Sagebrush Smith was startled by a fantastic sound. It was low, strange, and utterly exotic. *Trilling* best described it. Sagebrush at first made the mistake of thinking it was a product of the night wind and the desert sand, and only when he saw the apish Monk and the dapper "'Ham" peering at the bronze giant intently did he realize the latter must be making the sound—that it must be a small, unconscious habit. The note was low, indefinable, almost unearthly, and faded away into nothingness.

"This is Meander Surett's vault-steel chest," the bronze giant said.

"It sure answers the description he gave in his letter," Monk agreed.

"Monk, did you examine Meander Surett's desert laboratory closely?" asked the bronze man.

"We sure did," Monk said.

"Did it seem to you that Meander Surett could have been insane?"

"Insane?"

"That point is important. If the scientist was sane, his letter can be believed; in which case the man has made, beyond doubt, the greatest scientific discovery of ages."

"Think it's that important, huh?"

"Meander Surett's discovery, if genuine, cannot be estimated." The bronze man's unusual voice was serious. "The effects may change civilization, perhaps alter religions and overthrow governments. Results of a thing so unexpected and so startling are hard to estimate. The point is: Was Meander Surett sane—or did he only imagine he had made his fantastic discovery?"

Monk swallowed. He moistened his lips.

"Well," he said, "I think Meander Surett was sane."

"Ham," said the bronze man, "what do you think?"

"Nobody but a sane man could establish such a laboratory as he had," the dapper man replied. "But I also think he was out of his head from suffering for a while before he died—possibly for a few days, or maybe a few weeks."

The bronze giant looked at Sagebrush Smith. "What is your name?"

"Sagebrush Smith," said Sagebrush with involuntary haste.

THERE was something about this strange bronze man that gripped and compelled, and Sagebrush, who was indignant and wanted to stamp and shout and demand to know what it was all about, found that his tongue was falling over itself to give civil answers.

"Are you puzzled by all this?" the bronze man asked.

"Kinda," Sagebrush admitted.

"Here, briefly, is what has happened," the bronze man said. "A number of days ago a letter came to us in New York. It was from Meander Surett. It said that Meander Surett had worked for years in a secret Death Valley laboratory to perfect an amazing discovery. The nature of the discovery was revealed in the letter. But there was also a request that absolutely no one be told its nature. I am respecting Meander Surett's request for secrecy."

Sagebrush nodded and swallowed.

"Meander Surett's letter," continued the bronze man, "stated that unknown men had been trying to steal the discovery. Meander Surett confessed in the letter to killing one of these men, and also to capturing one, which he was holding prisoner.

"Monk and Ham came out here to investigate," the bronze man went on. "They found Meander Surett dead and buried. They radioed me to that effect, and I gave the information to the newspapers in such a manner that they did not know where it came from. There was no reason why it should be unknown that one of the greatest scientists of the day had died. And make no mistake—Meander Surett was a great scientist."

Sagebrush Smith nodded dumbly.

"Monk and Ham trailed you," the bronze man said. "They traced you to that ranch house. In the meantime, I had caught up with detail work in New York, and came out by plane to help personally with the investigation. Tonight Monk and Ham were to seize you and the metal box, while I went on into the desert to examine Meander Surett's laboratory. Suspecting there might be difficulties at the ranch, I delayed the desert trip, which explains my appearance a few minutes ago."

"I see," Sagebrush Smith said.

"Smith," said the bronze man, "why did you take that box?"

"Meander Surett gave it to me," Sagebrush explained. "He had me promise him to take it to his daughter Sally and Doc Savage."

"What was your opinion of Meander Surett's mental stability?"

"His what?"

"Was he crazy?"

"Hell, I don't know. He was, and he wasn't."

"What do you mean?"

"At first, I figured there was nothin' wrong with him," Sagebrush muttered. "He kept claimin' unknown people had been watchin' him. I thought maybe they had. But then he told me he'd caught one of the gents who was watchin' him, and had the geezer tied in the desert. When I looked, it was only a mangy coyote he had on a chain."

"A coyote?"

"Yeah. I—well, after that, I didn't know what to think."

For the second time, there came the faint trilling. The sound, Sagebrush decided, was one of the most eerie things he had ever heard.

The bronze man spoke to Monk and Ham. "You might as well head for the railroad with the cowboy and the box."

Monk said, "But——"

"I will go to Meander Surett's laboratory," the bronze man said. "It is of the utmost importance that we know whether or not his story was the product of a demented mind."

The bronze giant arose, moved aside a few yards and stood near a knobby gray clump of jumping cactus. Then, with weird abruptness, he had vanished.

SAGEBRUSH SMITH asked, "Who was that guy?"

"Doc," Monk said, "is Clark Savage, Jr., better known as Doc Savage, the man of bronze."

"Hm-m-m." Sagebrush rubbed his jaw thoughtfully. "So that's the gent they write about in the magazines so much."

"You sound a bit surprised," Monk growled.

"Kinda. I didn't figure there was no such hombre." Suddenly Sagebrush whacked his right fist into his left palm. "I still don't think," he yelled, "that he can hit fifty dimes in the air with fifty shots from a six-gun!"

"That," Monk said, "ain't no trick a-tall for Doc."

"You're a liar by the clock!" said Sagebrush. "There ain't no jasper can do such a thing!"

Monk grew indignant.

"Turn this guy's stern my way, Ham," he ordered.

"Why?" asked the dapper Ham.

"He's the hooligan who kicked me," Monk squawked. "I'm gonna reciprocate."

"I can lick both you jaspers!" said Sagebrush rashly.

Ham said to Monk, "You kick this man and I'll take this cane and carve a map of the moon on you. The moon is covered with craters, in case you don't know it, you hairy monstrosity!"

"Who's a hairy monstrosity?" demanded Monk irately.

"You. You're also a fur-encrusted gossoon, and as simple-witted as you look!"

"You keep that up," Monk said, "and I'll wring you out until you resemble your last year's gray spats!"

Sagebrush batted his eyes at them.

"You geezers seem to quarrel a little," he remarked.

Chapter V

SYMBOLS FOR TROUBLE

MONK and Ham stopped quarreling. Monk pointed at the moon.

"Look," he said.

A strange, gigantic insect seemed to be hanging in front of the moon, an insect with a fat body and a set of four wings which it whirled windmill fashion instead of flapping. The insect made a faint, hissing noise. It came nearer, sank close to the dry-wash in which Monk, Ham, and Sagebrush Smith crouched, and they could see the faint glow of light from an instrument panel.

"That ain't like no airplane I ever saw," Sagebrush Smith muttered.

"It's a true gyro," Ham advised him shortly. "One of the very few which ever got beyond the experimental stage. It can rise straight up, come straight down and hang absolutely motionless in the air."

"How does it do that?" Sagebrush demanded, not unreasonably.

"Go study aëronautical engineering for six years, Young Wild West," Monk advised, "and you'd understand it if it was explained to you."

"I can see," Sagebrush said, "that me and you are gonna get along great."

The gyro came to a dead stop overhead, the cabin window opened, and Doc Savage's arm appeared briefly and waved. Then the gyroplane's silenced motors hissed a little louder and it climbed straight up for a few hundred feet, after which the sound it made was almost inaudible. The gyro vanished out over the desert.

Doc Savage turned a knob and caused a hand to move around a dial which was marked with points of the compass. Then he turned switches, and a robot pilot took over the gyroplane and flew it on the compass course which he had set with the dial. Another dial-and-hand device governed the height.

From time to time, the bronze man changed the setting of this to keep close to the stony terrain below. In the space of a few miles, the sides of Death Valley sloped from an altitude of several thousand feet to below sea level.

The weirdness of Death Valley at night was spread below. Far to the right was the white smear of the great borax beds. They seemed ony a mile or two distant; were actually more than sixty miles away. Ahead, the Funeral Mountains reared; behind were the Panamint Mountains; and both ranges had a blackness that was a little fantastic.

Doc Savage consulted instruments which had nothing to do with the business at hand—a device for measuring cosmic penetration in this area, an apparatus for checking the characteristics of shorter radio waves at this lower-than-the-sea level. He filed the readings of the instruments for future reference—in his memory.

The bronze man had a prodigious memory, developed as a part of the remarkable two-hour routine of exercises which he had taken with daily regularity since childhood—exercises that accounted for many of his amazing faculties. He was continually experimenting, had a score of projects under way at times. It might be weeks before he got around to using the data he took from the instruments in Death Valley, but so highly was his memory trained that it would serve as well as a notebook.

Doc's next move was to spread old Meander Surett's letter in the glow from the instrument panel. The bronze man's training had made him skilled in many subjects, handwriting being one of them. He knew that it was possible to check the sanity of a person to an extent by the individual's handwriting.

But it was impossible to check old Meander Surett's

mental condition from his letter. The letter was typewritten, except for the signature. The signature was legible, and the letter text was rational enough.

The bronze man located Meander Surett's desert laboratory without difficulty. Monk and Ham had given him its location. Since the gyro did not need a runway to rise, as did an ordinary plane, he merely dropped it on the sand.

THE sand was white. In mounds and valleys and ridges and cones, it lay as albescent as bone dust. Jutting here and there, fantastic in the moonlight, was the scattered ruin of the prehistoric city, baffling physical presence of an enigma to scientists. There were other ruins on the floor of Death Valley, and they were as puzzling as this one.

Science knew something of the cliff dwellers of Arizona, the mound builders of the Mississippi valley, the pyramid-makers of Yucatan, because skeletons of the one-time inhabitants had been found. But the only skeletons ever found in these ruins had been those of prospectors who had died of heat that was almost a hundred and forty in the shade.

A sidewinder slid away sidewise, deadly blunt head and little eyes always on the bronze man. A little scorpion curled its stinger-bearing tail menacingly. Coyotes yapped in the distance, like children laughing. The little mouse-bodied bats of the desert floated close and made tiny noises with their teeth; sounds that were like one finger nail being picked with another finger nail.

Doc Savage reached the adobe hut which housed poor old Meander Surett's laboratory. He entered. When he turned a light switch, a motor-generator unit started and the place was flooded with luminance. He looked around.

Doc Savage himself maintained two laboratories—one in the New York skyscraper headquarters, the other in an isolated Arctic spot which he called his "fortress of Solitude." Both laboratories were remarkably complete. To the New York one came scientists from all over the world to examine, to copy the instruments developed there. The one in the Fortress of Solitude was even more complete, but only Doc Savage had ever seen it.

The bronze man spent three hours in old Meander

Surett's laboratory—for he knew he was examining something more complete than anything he had for research into the lesser-known phases of electrical phenomena.

He got out old Meander Surett's letter:

> The man was spying on me and tried to shoot me when I caught him, and I shot first with my rifle and killed him. He is buried one hundred yards due west of the door of my laboratory.

The bronze man frowned at that paragraph in the letter. Then he stepped off the hundred yards west of the adobe hut door and began digging.

The man buried there had, strangely enough, been mummified by the super-heated sand, probably because he had not been buried deep. He wore riding boots, khaki breeches, a khaki shirt. He had been shot squarely in the heart.

Old Meander Surett had buried his victim in haste. There was a bill fold in the man's inner coat pocket containing several hundred dollars in paper money.

The telegram was tucked inside the leather halves of the man's belt, which was composed of two strips of leather sewn together after the fashion of some belts. It would have escaped an ordinary search:

BILL HORDER
BARSTOW CALIFORNIA

IF YOU THINK HE HAS PERFECTED HIS DISCOVERY GO AHEAD AND GET HIM OUT OF THE WAY

There was no signature.

The envelope was tucked in the dead man's shirt pocket where any one could have found it. But it was empty, and no one would have been interested in it except a chemist or a pharmacist, who would know the meaning of the penciled symbols on the envelope. Doc Savage knew probably more chemistry than his aid, the homely Monk, who was one of the greatest contemporary industrial chemists.

The bullet which had killed the man was a .30-30 rifle bullet. Sagebrush Smith had not taken old Meander Surett's rifle. It was a .30-30.

Doc Savage made a large bundle of gunny sacks, canvas and waste from the laboratory. A container filled with paraffin would have been better. He fired the .30-30 into the rags, recovered the bullet and compared it with the one that had killed the man, using a pocket magnifier of considerable power.

Old Meander Surett might have kept a coyote chained in the desert under the impression it was a man, but it was also pretty evident that he had killed a man.

SAGEBRUSH SMITH had buried Meander Surett carefully and covered the body with stones lugged from the ruins which were all around and half buried in the desert sand. Atop the grave, the cowboy had erected a cross inscribed:

MEANDER SURETT

Scientist

Autopsies are not pleasant things. Doc Savage liked them no better than the next man, in spite of his intensive training as a surgeon which had brought him in contact with such things as dissecting rooms.

Meander Surett had not died from a cancer. His insides had been burned away by a pernicious poison, which had remained in his system and eaten and eaten until death had come.

The symbols on the envelope from the pocket of the man who had been shot was the formula of the poison which had killed Meander Surett.

So it was fairly evident that the man had poisoned the old scientist before the latter had caught him marauding and had killed him.

Doc Savage went back to the plane and turned on the short-wave radio.

"Monk," he said into the microphone.

There was a short wait. Monk and Ham would be keeping their portable short-wave outfit on monitor setting, only the receiver operating. The transmitter had to be switched on and warmed up.

Finally Monk's small voice could be heard saying, "—and I'm gonna slam you on the head, Ham, so hard that your ears will be growing out of your ankles." In a more pleasant tone, Monk said, "Yeah, Doc?"

"Meander Surett did not die from cancer," Doc Savage said. "He was poisoned. And he did kill a prowler, as his letter indicated."

"Then," Monk muttered, "it looks like he was sane."

"Meander Surett's death," Doc Savage said, "was obviously the result of a plot."

"Then maybe we'll run into some trouble on this yet," Monk remarked.

He sounded rather cheerful about the prospects.

"You will proceed back to New York," Doc Savage directed. "Does Sagebrush Smith wish to go?"

"I'll ask him," Monk grunted. "Hey, Young Wild West, do you wanta go to New York with us?"

The microphone was sensitive enough to bring Sagebrush Smith's response over the air to Doc Savage.

"I made old Meander Surett a promise and I'm gonna keep it, and don't think I ain't!" said Sagebrush.

"Yeah, but you've delivered the box to us," Monk reminded him.

"I ain't delivered it to Sally Surett," growled Sagebrush. "That was part of the bargain."

Monk said to Doc Savage. "He's a kind of contrary bonehead, Doc. Want me to tie a knot in his leg and leave him to untie it?"

"If he insists," Doc Savage said, "take him along."

"I insist!" Sagebrush yelled.

"If you go with us," Monk informed him, "you may get into trouble. We're generally kinda magnets for trouble."

"That's great," said Sagebrush. "I'd like to see what trouble is like."

"Doc, he ain't got no sense," Monk said.

"Gimme a gun," Sagebrush howled, "and then say that!"

Monk chuckled. "Doc, I think I'll give him a six-shooter and sic him on Ham."

Doc Savage said, "You can make it to the railroad by morning."

"What are you gonna do, Doc?"

"Some investigating," the bronze man explained, "in the direction of the Lazy Y ranch."

Chapter VI

BLOODHOUNDS FOR HIRE

AROUND the Lazy Y ranch house there was not exactly an air of jubilation. In fact, there was a good deal of wiping of perspiration from foreheads, passing around of a bottle which some one had produced from a tarp bed-roll, and puzzled discussion.

The Lazy Y hands had not figured out exactly what had happened. Those who had gone to sleep so mysteriously on the porch had awakened and been accused of playing possum. They had gotten scared and had all pretended to be dead, claimed the hands who had never left the bunk house.

The men then went out and gathered around the ripped corner of the ranch house, the shattered corral, the over-turned windmill, and the great pits in the ground, and asked each other a question:

"What done that?"

No one seemed to have been injured much.

Hoke McGee and the Lazy Y owner awakened after every one else.

"That sword cane had somethin' on it that put us to sleep," Hoke McGee muttered. "Where's Sagebrush and them other two ginks and that box?"

"Gone."

"You infernal cowards! You let 'em get away! Only three of 'em, and you let 'em get away!"

"There was more'n Sagebrush and the two others."

"How many more?"

"One more."

"One! Why, you buzzards! You let *one* hombre whip you all?"

"Somehow I ain't ashamed," a cowhand muttered. "Not when the one hombre was that bronze gent."

"Bronze?"

"He wasn't exactly a runt, either. He just walked up and made a remark kinda calmlike as if he was mentionin' the weather. Next thing you know, we didn't know nothin'."

"And the corner flew off the house, the windmill upset, the corral jumped to pieces, and the ground began to cough out chunks," another hand said.

HOKE MCGEE and the Lazy Y owner got a bottle of their own, locked themselves in the ranch house, sat at a table, and looked bewildered.

"That box," moaned Hoke, "weighed anyhow three hundred pounds. Figurin' it had two hundred and fifty pounds of gold in it, at thirty-five dollars an ounce, it would be worth a hundred and forty thousand dollars."

"You've got your troy and avoirdupois weights mixed up," mumbled the owner, "but it gives you some idea."

They sampled the bottle several times, but it did not help their spirits.

"We gotta call Everett Everett Barr," Hoke grumbled.

"Call him? Why? We want that chest of gold ourselves, don't we?"

"Look at it this way," Hoke said. "We ain't got no line on this thing, but Double-Everetts apparently has. He may be able to put us next to how we might head off the box."

This was logical, so Hoke McGee got on the telephone, which was fortunately in a part of the ranch house that was not ruined, and called Mr. Barr in New York City.

He told the whole sad story substantially as he understood it had happened, neglecting, however, to mention that he'd held private designs on the box's contents.

"That's bad, Hoke, old boy, old socks, old kid," said Everett Everett Barr. "Er—describe your Nemesis again, will you?"

"My what?"

"The—oh—personage of bronze who put your men to sleep."

"I didn't see him," Hoke growled, "but from reports, he was somethin' that just couldn't be."

"In that case," said Everett Everett Barr sadly, "there's no doubt about who he was."

"Eh?"

"Doc Savage."

"Who," Hoke asked, "is Doc Savage?"

The inquiry seemed to astonish Everett Everett Barr beyond belief. "Hoke, old buddy," he said, "who invented the phonograph?"

"Thomas A. Edison," Hoke said.

"And who is president of the United States?"

"Theodore—I mean, Franklin Roosevelt."

"And who discovered America?"

"Christopher Columbus," said Hoke. "What the blazes has that got to do with it?"

"Nothing," Mr. Barr said, "except that I am amazed that you have heard of those persons and not of Doc Savage."

HOKE MCGEE realized that Everett Everett Barr was very earnest about this.

"Well," Hoke said, "I never heard of any Doc Savage. What's he a doctor of?"

"Trouble."

"Eh?"

"Other people's troubles, perhaps I should have said." Mr. Barr cleared his throat. "Hoke, my trusty friend, my valued colleague, this Doc Savage is one of the most remarkable men the world has known. You have heard of the mythical City of To-morrow, the ultramodern metropolis of the future? Doc Savage is the Man of To-morrow. He is a combination of scientific genuis, muscular marvel and Sir Galahad. He is to-day what they hope man will be a few centuries in the future. He is an electrician, chemist, geologist, engineer, surgeon and I don't know what else. Mind you, he's *not* just an ordinary electrician, chemist and so on. He's probably the best there is in any and all these lines."

"Yeah?"

"Furthermore," Mr. Barr continued, "Doc Savage has

five assistants who are world-noted scientists, engineers and lawyers. They make a formidable company, believe you me. Two of them, Monk, the chemist, and Ham, the lawyer, were evidently with him to-night at your ranch!"

"Yeah?" Hoke said.

"Anything," Mr. Barr declared, "that interests Doc Savage to the point where he came all the way to Death Valley is bound to be big."

"I see," Hoke said.

"Very big indeed." Everett Everett Barr smacked his lips. "And I happen to know this is big. Yes, I do. I know certain details which even Doc Savage does not know and which, if he did know them, would doubtless cause him to be rather excited. And I understand he does not excite easily."

"You mean you know somethin' about that box?"

"Indeed I do, Hoke, old pard, old chum, old soak, old——"

"Who's payin' for this call?" Hoke interrupted.

"Why—er—you are, aren't you?"

"In that case," Hoke snarled, "I don't wanta discuss somebody named Doc Savage. And never mind so much 'old-chum, old-pal' stuff. How we gonna get hold of that box again?"

"They will doubtless head for the nearest town," Mr. Barr said, "where they will take a train to Los Angeles, where they will get a plane for New York."

"Plane?"

"Doc Savage cannot take the box and his men back in his airship because he is flying a gyroplane which cannot lift that much weight. The gyro is a small ship, and the only one of its kind in the world."

"You seem to know a lot about Doc Savage's being out here," Hoke muttered.

Everett Everett Barr chuckled.

"Hoke, old son," he said, "I have been right on this job for months. I knew Doc Savage might be summoned by old Meander Surett. I knew it because old Surett's letters to his daughter—um—I mean, his letters—ah—his letters were all postmarked Los Angeles.

"Some months ago, I employed a man named Bill Horder, who located Meander Surett. Bill Horder and myself—ah—had plans for Meander Surett. But something happened and I did not hear from Bill Horder again. Unfortunately, I did not know where to find Meander Surett until I read that he had been found dead in Death Valley. Of course, I got in touch with you right away."

Hoke digested that for some moments.

"Just what's behind this?" he demanded.

"You can't imagine."

"Blast it, of course not!" Hoke snapped. "That's why I'm askin'!"

"What I meant is that it is so big you couldn't imagine the possibilities," said Mr. Barr. "It's stupendous. It's—ah—colossal. Hoke, old prince, stick with me and you'll be a millionaire. Why, bless me, a billionaire, maybe!"

"I'm askin' you," Hoke said, "what's in that box?"

"You bring the box to me," said Mr. Barr, "and I'll show you, and also give you twenty-five thousand dollars, and later a lot more money."

"But——"

"Instead of wasting words," added Mr. Barr, "suppose you be heading after the box?"

Hoke McGee hung up and contemplated the telephone disgustedly for some time. Then he got out makings and constructed himself a somewhat droopy cigarette.

"You know what?"

"What?" asked the Lazy Y owner.

"I'm beginnin' to think there's somethin' besides gold in that box," Hoke muttered.

THE cowhand who dashed into the Lazy Y ranch house a few minutes later was excited.

"Hey!" he exploded. "We thought we saw that bronze feller again!"

"Where?" yelled Hoke.

"Walkin' out there in the mesquite."

"Was he near the house?"

"Naw. He couldn't get close. We been keepin' a close lookout."

Hoke relaxed. "I guess he couldn't 'a' heard nothin'," he muttered.

It was about this time that Doc Savage was returning to an equipment case a sensitive electrical device which enabled him to eavesdrop on a telephone wire from a distance of a score or more yards. He had not been near the Lazy Y ranch house, but he had been under the telephone line while Hoke McGee was talking to Everett Everett Barr.

Chapter VII

DETOUR

SAGEBRUSH SMITH had never been a young man who was readily impressed. There were few things which ever had held him spellbound. The Grand Canyon of the Colorado had done so, on the one occasion he had seen it. Sometimes the panoramic vastness and the eerie character of Death Valley held him silent and awed. He refused to be spellbound by Doc Savage, the mystery surrounding one metal box, or two strange fellows named Monk and Ham.

However, Sagebrush was somewhat impressed by two animals named Habeas Corpus and Chemistry which turned up in the dry-wash.

Habeas Corpus was a pig, and a remarkable pig. A shote with legs as long as those of a dog, ears that came nigh being wings, and a long, inquisitive snout. Habeas was Monk's pet.

Chemistry was a source of doubt in Sagebrush Smith's mind, because Chemistry probably could be an orang-outang, baboon, or runt gorilla. There was room for argument. The animal might have been a combination of any number of branches of the monkey family. Chemistry was dapper Ham's pet.

"Haw! Haw! Haw!" whooped Sagebrush gleefully.

"What's eatin' you, Jesse James?" Monk demanded.

"Every time I see that Chemistry thing," Sagebrush chortled, "he looks more like you!"

"The time is comin' closer," Monk said, "when I take one cowboy in my two hands and squeeze and there will just be a little grease on my hands and no cowboy."

"You're quite a bag of wind," Sagebrush grinned.

Monk fished a silver half dollar from his pocket, held it between thumb and fingers, squeezed slowly—and bent the half dollar neatly double. He surveyed the result and seemed disappointed.

"Generally I squeeze 'em back into nuggets," he explained.

Sagebrush Smith swallowed. It was an incredible feat of strength, and he was impressed with the fact that Monk was apparently as strong as the bull ape which he resembled.

"All muscle and no brains," Sagebrush muttered.

The remark seemed to anger dapper Ham. He pointed his cane at Sagebrush.

"I'll tell you something Two-gun Terror," he said. "Monk is one of the greatest chemists in the world."

Sagebrush sniffed. "I guess Doc Savage has to have somebody around to do the muscle work."

Monk scowled. "Listen, Six-shooter Sam," he growled, "I had to use the strength of my whole hand to bend that half dollar. *Doc can do it with his little finger!*"

"Bunk," Sagebrush said, a trifle uncertainly.

"You'll see," Monk promised him.

Eventually they reached the town of Barstow, and Sagebrush Smith provided himself with a suit of store clothes, a new pair of cowboy boots and a cheap suitcase. About the time he finished shopping, a passenger train came in and they got aboard. Habeas and Chemistry were placed in the baggage car.

Hoke McGee reached town just in time to swing, unobserved, aboard the last coach of the same train. With Hoke were half a dozen Lazy Y hands who were what is known in Western parlance as gun-slicks.

THE train was streamlined, and it rumbled across the desert like a jointed metal worm, pursued by a rope of dust. Heat shimmered in waves off the sides of the cars, danced weirdly over the desert and blended with changing mirages.

When the train was nearing Los Angeles, the man in the khaki uniform appeared. He had white hair, rather staring eyes of a brilliant blue color and a tobacco-stained white mustache of the kind usually called a "soup-strainer." He walked always with a stoop, and his garments were ill-fitting; probably he would have been very large had he straightened.

"Disinfection before you enter Los Angeles county," he announced.

"Disinfection?" muttered Hoke McGee. "What's disinfection?"

"I don't know," said a puncher, "but I think it's what they do when you're lousy."

"I resent that!" said Hoke McGee.

Resent it or not, he submitted meekly to being led back to the men's washroom.

"Just take off your coat, shirt and undershirt," directed the old man with the white hair and brilliant blue eyes.

Scowling, Hoke McGee complied. The white-haired man produced a sponge and a bottle of amber liquid. He dampened the sponge with the liquid and gave Hoke McGee's back, chest, and arms a sponge bath.

"That's all," the blue-eyed man said. "It's just a health measure."

Hoke McGee went back to his seat, sat down and rubbed his jaw.

"There wasn't much to it," he admitted.

He watched the rest of his Lazy Y gun-slicks being escorted back to the wash room, one at a time, where they were sponged, then allowed to don their shirts and coats and return to their seats.

Hoke was considerably less concerned when he observed that all the other male passengers were being taken back to the wash room one at a time. This disinfecting, he decided, was some new project of the Democrats in Washington.

"Still, this disinfectin' is a new one on me," he muttered.

Hoke's mind would have not been so placid had he known that the other passengers were not sponged. They were merely asked a few questions about past ailments and permitted to return to their seats.

The coach occupied by Hoke McGee and his men was the only one in which the blue-eyed man conducted his "disinfecting" operations. When the blue-eyed man had finished with that coach, he went forward to a drawing room in one of the Pullmans. He unwrapped tissue paper from a small object which came out of a pocket.

It was a small suction cup equipped with a handle, and he applied this carefully to one eye, then the other, and removed the blue glass caps which had disguised the flake gold hue of his eyes. He took off the gray mustache. He applied a chemical cleaner to his hair and eradicated the white hue, exposing the natural dark bronze color.

Having removed his disguise, Doc Savage changed to a subdued dark business suit, then glanced into the club car. Monk, Ham, and Sagebrush Smith were riding there, and old Meander Surett's vault-steel chest was beside them.

Doc Savage went back to his drawing room without revealing his presence on the train. Doc aids did not know he was aboard, for after hiding his gyroplane in the desert the bronze man had followed them aboard, fearing Hoke McGee might attempt some trickery and to keep an eye on him and his men.

MONK was occupying the time trying to explain to Sagebrush Smith just how remarkable an individual was Doc Savage.

"You're tryin' to make it sound," Sagebrush said, "like Doc Savage gets mixed up in stranger things than anybody else."

"Did you ever hear about the time Doc found that lost island of prehistoric dinosaurs?" Monk demanded.

"Naw."

"Ever hear of the devilish goings-on we found in the Louisiana swamps?"

"Nope."

"Or about how Doc got his start?"

"No."

"You're practically uneducated," Monk said.

"What gets me," grumbled Sagebrush, "is why Doc Savage should be stickin' his nose in this."

"Look, Billy the Kid," Monk explained, "Doc got a letter."

"Sure. But why did Meander Surett write him?"

"It's this way," Monk said patiently. "Doc Savage was trained from childhood to follow a career of righting wrongs and punishing evil-doers in all parts of the world. I thought everybody knew that until I ran into you."

"These aspersions you're castin' on my education," said Sagebrush, "is gonna get your nose skinned for you."

"I'll help you skin his nose," volunteered the dapper Ham. "What'll we do with the hide?"

"My idea would be to use it to make a muffler for you!" Sagebrush said belligerently.

Ham frowned. Monk grunted. Sagebrush Smith glared at the pair.

"You gents ain't explained," he reminded, "why Meander Surett wrote Doc Savage to begin with."

"Meander Surett wanted his discovery to benefit mankind," Monk said. "He knew Doc would see that it did. You'd savvy that if you wasn't so donkey-eared."

"What's in the steel box, short-and-hairy?" Sagebrush asked.

"That's a secret."

"Who's got the key?"

"Doc. It was enclosed in Meander Surett's letter."

"There's too durn much mystery about this!" Sagebrush complained. "I'm plumb puzzled."

"Maybe the texture of your head has got somethin' to do with that," Monk said.

"For two bits," stated Sagebrush heatedly, "I'd take the box and go hunt Sally Surett and let you ginks go twiddle your thumbs!"

"Any time you get that box away from us," Monk said, "you'll be a lot wiser than you are to-day."

"Yeah?" growled the cowboy.

"Yeah!" Monk said.

Sagebrush Smith was sensitive about having reflections cast on his education. Doubtless this was because his schooling had stopped at the third grade. However, he had read a great deal and rightfully considered himself rather well versed. He was not dumb.

Sagebrush began to be possessed of a hot desire to show Monk and Ham that he was not dumb.

SAGEBRUSH SMITH had never ridden on a railroad train, but he didn't let this faze him. It was the automobile age anyhow. Moreover, he'd been up in an airplane, although that was a number of years ago when a barnstormer in an old Jenny had set down at Tonopah one time to hop passengers at ten dollars per, and hold your own hat.

Railroad travel turned out to be about what he had expected, although he hadn't thought it would be as comfortable as it was in the air-conditioned coaches.

They arrived in Los Angeles. Unnoticed by any one, Doc Savage got off the train and disappeared in the crowd.

Los Angeles was much more than Sagebrush had expected. He was indignant when Monk and Ham wouldn't let him do what he called, "throw a little toot in this place." They went out to the airport at once, to his disgust.

Aviation, Sagebrush perceived, had changed somewhat since he had last been up in a plane. Great ships dropped onto the airport tarmac, took off, or were snaked in and out of hangars by grumbling caterpillar tractors.

Sagebrush watched an air liner taxi up to the passenger canopy and unload.

"Holy litters!" he said. "There was anyway thirty-five people got outta that thing!"

"There'll be that many on the one we ride to New York, Cole Younger," Monk said. "Get that there box and have it weighed and put on the plane."

Sagebrush scowled.

"Another thing," he gritted, "you better quit callin' me them wild west names and givin' me orders!"

Sagebrush disappeared into the baggage room. Monk stood outside and watched the doors, just on the chance that Sagebrush might try to skip out with the box. However, Monk grinned as he kept a lookout; he rather liked the belligerent cow-puncher, and believed Sagebrush was perfectly honest. But the salty cow-puncher might try to put something over on them, just to show that he could do it.

While Monk watched, Ham bought and paid for their airline tickets to New York. Then they joined Sagebrush Smith in the baggage room.

"What the dickens!" Monk exploded.

Sagebrush Smith was knotting a rope around a canvas-covered object the size of the vault-steel chest. He finished tying a granny knot and gave the rope a jerk, then straightened and wiped off perspiration.

"I put some canvas around the box," he said. "Figured it mightn't do no harm to disguise it."

"That's not a bad idea, considering the source." Monk pointed at the rope. "But such knots! How you gonna untie 'em? Why don't you tie sailor knots?"

"Them's cowboy knots," Sagebrush explained. "A cowboy always carried a knife."

They carried the box, grunting and stumbling, to a truck, and saw it loaded aboard the plane they were to take. A few minutes later the public-address system of the airport announced that it was time for passengers to get aboard. There was some argument about letting the pets on board—until Monk told who they were.

Sagebrush Smith was first on the big air liner.

"Kinda like a kid," Monk chuckled.

MONK and Ham were seasoned air travelers who had flown more miles than they had kept track of, and they stood back and watched the other passengers enter. Monk watched the feminine passengers in particular.

Monk had an eye for the ladies, and long ago he had discovered that his ludicrous homeliness, combined with the fact that he had a pet pig, somehow made it easy for him to get started with the ladies.

Ham occupied his time scowling at Monk and making biting cracks about the homely chemist. No one could recall ever having heard Monk and Ham speak a civil word to each other, although there had been occasions when each had risked his life for the other. Usually, their association was a continual quarrel. But Sagebrush Smith had been so quarrelsome that he had interfered with their private squabble. They were behind on their dirty digs.

Monk developed a great grin.

"There goes Mary Main, the movie queen," he chortled. "I bet I have her dated up before we get to New York."

They climbed into the plane, and as they passed the movie charmer's seat, Ham spoke.

"Why, Monk Mayfair," he said loudly, "isn't your charming wife going with you this trip?"

Monk shuffled to his seat and collapsed into it.

"You—you—toad in fine feathers!" he gritted. "Now she'll think I'm married! I'm gonna dump you out to feed the first buzzards we see!"

The two became fully occupied with a quarrel.

They were so occupied that the plane was in the air and had flown a hundred miles before Monk lifted his head and sniffed. He wrinkled his nose.

"What's that smell?" he muttered.

The aroma had not been noticeable at first, but during the last few minutes it had become quite perceptible.

"Must be a polecat in here," Monk hazarded.

Ham looked at Monk. "As long as I've associated with it, strange I never noticed its odor before."

Monk passed that insult because something had occurred to him. He sprang out of his seat and dashed forward. A moment later he tore past Ham, making for the stern. He came back, scowl wrinkles creasing his minimum of a forehead.

"We still got the chest, at least," he muttered.

"What's that got to do with the smell, Ignatz?" Ham demanded.

"Sagebrush Smith," said Monk, "has skedaddled."

"What?"

"Gone." Monk squared out a pair of hairy fists. "I dunno what the smell is. Blast that cow-chaperon! He musta gone in the front door of this thing, then climbed outta one of them little doors in the pilot's compartment."

"While you were looking for women!" Ham sneered.

"We gotta have this plane turn back," Monk yelled. "He won't get away with this!"

The two pilots of the passenger air liner had different ideas about turning back. They had a schedule to make, they pointed out. They would turn back for a storm, but not on the whim of a couple of irate passengers.

"But I'm Lieutnant Colonel Andrew Blodgett Mayfair!" Monk shouted.

So what? He could be second cousin to the sultan of Timbuctoo, and still so what? Ham might be Brigadier General Theodore Marley Brooks, as he stated, and so what? Furthermore, what was that smell in the plane? They were Doc Savage's assistants? The pilots swallowed.

One picked up his radio mike and called his ground

station, explaining that two of Doc Savage's men were aboard and wanted to turn back. He listened intently to the reply.

"That makes it different," he said. He called the stewardess. "Tell the passengers that we are turning back to Los Angeles, but that nothing is wrong."

The stewardess went back down the aisle telling the seat occupants—some of whom were holding their noses by now—that nothing was wrong.

FOUR men evidently did not believe her. These four men had weather-beaten faces and grim expressions, and after they got to their feet, they had guns in their hands. Big, worn guns which looked as if they had seen use. They were Hoke McGee and three of his best men who had been keeping well hidden behind newspapers.

"Get 'em up!" Hoke McGee roared. "This is a holdup!"

This was one of the new sound-proofed planes and their words carried. Their guns were also rather convincing. Hands began lifting.

Ham and Monk found themselves looking into gun snouts. With alacrity, their arms arose.

"Now," Monk said, "I know the source of the fragrance in here!"

"Where's that box?" Hoke McGee demanded.

"It ain't aboard," Monk said unblushingly.

Hoke McGee snorted. "I just wondered how convincin' a lie you could tell," he chuckled. "I seen 'em put it on the ship."

One of the Lazy Y gun-slicks had gone forward and disarmed the pilot and co-pilot who had guns because the ship carried mail.

Hoke McGee and another man entered the baggage compartment and wrestled the heavy canvas-covered case out into the cabin. Hoke broke his finger nails on Sagebrush Smith's knots, then used his jackknife. He threw back the canvas.

"Damn!" he croaked.

Monk felt like making it stronger. He popped his eyes at the old square trunk full of brickbats which the canvas had covered. Ham gave Monk a jab in the ribs.

"That infernal cowboy," he groaned. "He put one over on us!"

Hoke McGee overheard the remark. Hoke began swearing. He swore for a long period without once repeating himself.

"We gotta go back and get on Sagebrush Smith's trail again!" he snarled.

The pilots, menaced by the blue-black eye of a gun, turned the plane back. They followed Hoke McGee's directions about where to make a landing.

Evidently Hoke was all prepared for a get-away with the chest he hadn't got. The plane had hardly stopped rolling on the desert near Los Angeles where it landed when a touring car pulled out of the brush and drew alongside.

Hoke McGee stabbed his gun menacingly at Monk and Ham.

"The next time you jiggers cross my trail!" he roared, "I'm gonna ventilate you plenty!"

Then he ran to the car and got in. They took the pilot and his assistant, carried them four miles down the desert road and threw them out. Then they drove furiously toward Los Angeles. The car's occupants held to anything that was handy, swayed with the bucking of the machine, and at times made small, involuntary gestures as if they wanted to hold their noses.

The driver looked around. "Have you gents noticed a kind of funny smell?" he demanded.

"There ain't nothin' funny about it!" Hoke McGee snarled.

"What is it?"

"That," Hoke said, "is what I'm wonderin'!"

Chapter VIII

THE BLOND SALLY SURETT

SAGEBRUSH SMITH was as tickled as he had been at any time in his life. He was in stitches; his ribs were hurting from laughing.

He had been standing outside the window of the radio room at the airport and the window was open, and he had heard the hubbub when Monk and Ham had demanded that the plane turn back, so Sagebrush knew Monk and Ham had learned that he was missing. He hoped they knew he had swapped boxes on them, too.

Now he was waiting for further word from the plane; as a matter of fact, he had decided to wait until Monk and Ham came back, then he would join them with the genuine box. He believed he would get more respect.

"I showed 'em they wasn't so slick," he chuckled.

A commotion inside the radio room drew his attention. An attendant dashed out and returned shortly with some one higher up.

"What's happened?" the higher-up demanded.

"The plane carrying Doc Savage's men has been hijacked!" the radio operator shouted. "Four cowboys under the leadership of a man named Hoke McGee made it land in the desert. They were after a box of some kind. The pilot and co-pilot were carried away by the robbers. Doc Savage's man named Monk is giving us details over the plane's radio."

There was more excited talk, but it was only meat on the skeleton of the event as first outlined.

Sagebrush Smith did not feel like laughing. He rubbed his jaw, considering. It appeared he had unwittingly thwarted a robbery; in taking the vault-steel case, he had kept it out of Hoke McGee's hands.

"Well, rawhide my bronc!" he muttered. "I really done the best thing that I could've done!"

Very well pleased with himself, Sagebrush ambled into the waiting room. As long as there was a robber scare, he didn't see any sense in being caught loitering suspiciously near radio room windows.

He was leaning on the counter inspecting a plane time table when he saw the platinum blonde girl.

It just happened that this was the first platinum blond girl Sagebrush Smith had ever seen. Also the first time he had seen in the flesh the kind of feminine figure the movies liked to feature. The combination rather took the cowhand's breath. He fund himself swallowing to maintain equilibrium.

The blonde startler tapped up to the ticket window on high heels.

"I wish to charter a plane," she declared.

"Ah—where do you wish to fly to?" asked the attendant.

The blonde girl was twisting a black leather purse and black suede gloves nervously with her hands. Her attire was black, the color which brought out her shimmering silver blondness and peach complexion as a dark velvet background brings out the facets of a diamond.

"My father," she said in a low voice, "has been found dead at his laboratory in Death Valley. I wish to rent a plane and a pilot to fly me to the spot."

"I see," said the attendant.

"I just arrived from New York by plane," the blond girl continued. "I left New York as soon as I read about my father's death in the newspapers."

Sagebrush Smith took several deep swallows and got hold of his wits. He addressed the girl.

"I—er—I'll bet—say, this is quite a coincidence," he said.

The blond beauty looked at him coolly. "I beg your pardon."

Sagebrush flushed uncomfortably.

"I beg yours, too," he mumbled. "Ah—er—are you Sally Surett?"

"Why, yes," the girl said curiously. "How did you know?"

SAGEBRUSH SMITH was having more difficulty than he had hitherto experienced in conducting a conversation.

"Why, I—uh—that is," he said. "Well—uh—this is some coincidence. I found your old—er—I am the man who found your father as he was dyin'."

The blond girl winced a little, then frowned. "I thought the person or persons who found my father had refused to reveal their identity," he said.

Sagebrush squirmed. He had never been able to carry on a coherent conversation with a girl, even a very plain one.

"It's kind of funny—I mean—it's a queer story," he mumbled. "It's as mud as clear—uh—it's as clear as mud, that is. Your father shot a prowler, but he had a coyote chained—and—well, I don't—anyhow, I've got the box."

"You're not making it very understandable," the girl said.

"I—uh—ain't used to girls as pretty as you," Sagebrush said. Which was a gallantry of high order, even if accidental.

The blond looked at him. She decided to smile.

"Maybe if we sat in chairs over there," she said, "you could get used to me."

Sagebrush had done a little thinking by the time they were settled in a chair. He turned cautious.

"Er—can you prove you are old Meander Surett's daughter?" he asked.

She could. She did. At least, there was a birth certificate, automobile driver's license for New York State, and numbers of letters addressed to Sally Surett, 110 North Boulevard, New York City. Sagebrush was satisfied.

It took him twenty minutes to explain all that had happened. Whenever he looked at the blond girl, his sentences came apart and he had to take out time to put them together. He finished at last and Sally Surett looked at him. She had big blue eyes that gave out electric shocks.

"I think you're marvelous," she said.

Sagebrush thought she was marvelous. He didn't think the world was such a bad place either.

"I—uh——" he said. "That is—well—oh, gosh!"

A voice behind Sagebrush Smith said, "There he is!"

Another voice, a squeaky one, said, "Make room, because I'm gonna pat him on the floor."

Sagebrush peered at Monk and Ham, who looked as though they wanted to relieve him of arms and legs. Behind them came their pets.

"Er—meet Miss Sally Surett," Sagebrush said.

Monk and Ham stopped. Monk was the first to get off his hat. Sally Surett had the type of blonde beauty which had a devastating effect on Monk.

"Not the great Meander Surett's daughter?" he asked in a properly awed tone.

"Yes," the blonde vision admitted.

Ham said, "Er—ahem! I am Brigadier General Theodore Marley Brooks and——"

"Better known as Ham," Monk interrupted. "It's too bad you can't meet—*yeoow!*"

Ham had kicked a patch of hide off Monk's ankle.

"What Monk started to say," said Ham politely, "is that it is too bad you can't meet his wife, Mrs. Blodgett Mayfair, and some of their numerous children."

"You shyster!" Monk gritted.

"You'd be interested in the children, I'm sure," Ham said. "All, unfortunately, look like their sire. Cutest collection of little apes you ever saw."

MONK and Ham spluttered at each other. They wanted to cultivate Sally Surett, ask her about her father's discovery, give Sagebrush Smith a clubbing, and fight each other. While they made irate noises, Sagebrush Smith spoke.

"I have the box in the express room here at the airport," he said.

Sally Surett took his arm.

"I'd love to see it," she murmured. "Good day," she said to Monk and Ham. "Nice to have met you."

"Er—we're not leaving just yet," Monk said foolishly.

They went to the baggage room, where Sagebrush

Smith grinningly dragged a canvas-covered case from the corner. The cowboy could not repress a gloat.

"I reckon it's sure lucky I swapped boxes," he said.

Monk and Ham said nothing. The only thing they could say was that it had indeed been lucky, and they didn't want to give Sagebrush that much satisfaction.

"Do take the cover off," the blond girl murmured.

Sagebrush Smith whipped out his jackknife, cut the ropes with a flourish and threw back the canvas. Then he looked as if he had walked over the rim of a canyon. He almost fell down. There was just an old wooden box filled with bricks.

"Gee whizz!" Sagebrush said miserably.

The blond girl looked bewildered. "But I thought the chest was of a steel which couldn't be cut with torches!"

"It is," Sagebrush groaned.

"But——" She frowned. "I don't understand."

"Me neither," the cowboy gulped.

"If I wasn't so disgusted," Monk said, "I'd conduct me a one-cowboy massacre on the spot."

"Do you mean that some one took the chest from *you?*" the girl demanded of Sagebrush.

"It sure looks powerful like it," Sagebrush confessed.

It was Ham, withdrawing in aloof disgust to stand twirling his dark cane, who noticed a mark on the baggage room wall. He stepped closer and scrutinized the mark. It was a series of figures, which might have been put there by some one who had carelessly totaled up a sum on the wall.

"Pull the shades," Ham said briefly.

Monk stared at Ham, and his homely face lighted. He hurried to draw the shades. It became gloomy in the room.

From one pocket, Ham extracted a flat device the length and width of the leather cases used to carry cigars, but deeper, and equipped with a folding crank after the fashion of pocket movie cameras which operated a tiny generator inside the device. There was a lens on the apparatus, a lens almost black in color.

Ham turned the crank vigorously while pointing the device at the wall where he had found the figures. The contrivance was a portable projector of ultra-violet light. The ultra-violet rays, invisible to the unaided eye, struck the wall and caused a fluorescence of words written there with a chalk which Doc Savage had perfected. The chalk, like such common substances as aspirin and vaseline, fluoresced or glowed under ultra-violet light.

The message read:

> Have taken box to Surfside Hotel to conduct examination.

"But who wrote that?" Sagebrush Smith demanded excitedly.

"Doc," Monk said. "He must have been sticking close to us and keeping track of that thing."

IT was a simple matter to get a taxi-cab at the airport. Monk, Ham, Sagebrush Smith and the blond girl loaded aboard, along with the pets. Chemistry rode in front with the driver. Habeas stayed in the back with Monk. The hack driver said that he ought to know where the Surfside Hotel was because it was one of the best in the city.

At first, every one in the cab was rather quiet, the natural reaction of persons who had just received a shaking-up. Then Ham frowned at his black cane and spoke.

"Your father's letter," he told Sally Surett, "indicated he had written you about the contents of that case."

"Oh, yes," said the young woman. "He wrote me a great many times."

Sagebrush Smith came to life. "What is in the case?" he demanded.

The blond girl smiled at him in a way that was highly disturbing. "I'll show you," she said. To their driver, she called, "Stop the cab! I wish to buy a newspaper."

She spread the newspaper out for Monk, Ham and Sagebrush to see.

They stared at the headlines with profound astonishment.

SURETT INVENTED "SPIRIT RADIO" DEVICE
COMPLETED BEFORE DEATH

Proved "Static" Is From Spirit World
Machine Translates It

The dream of spiritualists and ordinary mankind from the beginning of time has come true, according to an announcement made by Sally Surett, daughter of the great scientist, Meander Surett, who was lately found dead near his Death Valley laboratory.

Part of the so-called "static" heard on an ordinary radio is an effort by beings on the astral plane to get in touch with living humans, Miss Surett said her father had proved conclusively.

Miss Surett, a striking blonde, is enroute to Los Angeles to charter a plane to visit her father's laboratory.

"Thomas A. Edison, the great inventor, first worked on the theory that the little-known forms of static might be spirit messages," said Miss Surett. "My father carried on from that start."

Former associates of Thomas A. Edison, when interviewed, admitted that Miss Surett's statement was true.

"Blazes!" Monk said. "I didn't dream—that is—why—*blazes!*"

Ham stared at Sally Surett. "You gave this interview to the newspapers?"

"Of course."

"Why?"

"Why not?"

That stumped Doc's aids. They could not think of any reason why Sally Surett should not have given an interview to the press. They were conscious that she was waiting for them to state a reason for opposing the giving out of information; they had the impression that that she was disapproving.

"I sure can't see no reason for it bein' a big secret," said Sagebrush Smith. "It wasn't my idea."

The young woman smiled at the cowboy gratefully. Then she looked coolly at Monk and Ham.

"I just wonder," she said frostily, "if these gentlemen and Doc Savage could have some ulterior motive in wishing this to be kept quiet."

"I dunno what an ulterior motive is, exactly," said Sagebrush, "but I wouldn't be surprised."

Chapter IX

DIFFERENCE OF OPINION

THE Hotel Surfside was as flustered as a prim old maid trying to entertain a football team. The Surfside ordinarily sailed along as placidly as the Indian dugout canoes which are to be found in museums. It was a hostelry which prided itself on nothing happening.

The Surfside was very strict about this nothing-happening policy, which was pursued on direct orders from the management in New York. Just the night before, a prominent lawyer had been thrown out of the bar for singing six words of "Sweet Adeline." As for motion picture people, they weren't even permitted to register.

They hadn't intended to permit Doc Savage to register. No indeed! The clerk had heard of Doc Savage, the man of bronze who was always fighting somebody's war. But after Doc Savage presented a document, the clerk stopped explaining that the New York management was particular about the guests. The document said that Doc Savage *was* the New York management! The clerk hadn't known that. He did everything but get down on his knees and bump his forehead on the floor.

The bronze man was calm about it and merely asked for a suite where he would not be disturbed. He also requested that several metal cases which had come by air express from New York consigned to a Mr. Clark be sent to the suite. He explained that they contained his equipment.

The bronze man had been carrying a metal box, and when three bell boys insisted on helping him with it, he let them do so.

That was four hours ago and the bell boys were now standing in the lobby telling each other how heavy the steel box had been, and how Doc Savage had handled it so easily with one hand. One bell hop wanted to bet it weighed five hundred pounds; an exaggeration, of course.

The rest of the bell boys were quietly moving the guests off the floor which held Doc Savage's suite. The bronze man had said he wanted privacy, and he was going to get it; the Surfside prided itself on giving service in large letters.

The clerk was leaning on the desk downstairs, rubbing his jaw and thinking. He could recall, back during the depression when the hotel had been about to fail and throw every one out of work, that had been taken over by what was known only as the Eastern Management.

At the time, some remarkably sensible suggestions had come from the Eastern Management as to what policies to follow; as a result, the hotel had been prosperous since. The clerk grinned. He was remembering, too, that he had heard that Doc Savage had taken over other near-failing industries—factories, stores, a steamship line or two, even a railroad, and by some magical business touch—probably common sense—had kept them going so that no one had lost any jobs.

The clerk's musings were interrupted when one very pretty blond girl, three concerned men, one pig and one runt ape entered the lobby. Sally Surett, Monk, Ham, Sagebrush, Habeas Corpus and Chemistry made a unique group.

"I am very sorry," the clerk said instantly, "but we do not take theatrical guests."

The dapper Ham frowned at Monk.

"We should have left you outside," he said. "Then he wouldn't have mistaken us for sideshow freaks."

Monk smacked the desk with a hairy fist. "We're assistants to Doc Savage!" he squeaked. "Where's Doc?"

"Oh," the clerk said. "I beg your pardon."

Doc Savage stood beside a long table in a room where the furniture was substantial enough to be practical, but not practical enough to be ugly. It was a comfortable, homey room, yet it seemed to emphasize the remarkable physical power of the bronze man.

He had removed his coat and tie, and rolled up his shirt sleeves. From across the room, the development of his forearms seemed ordinary, but when the new arrivals came close, cabled layers of sinew were subtly evident under fine-textured bronze skin.

The tall blond girl stopped suddenly when she saw the bronze man at close range. He affected people that way.

"Doc, this is Sally Surett," Monk said.

The blond girl advanced, holding out her hand, turning on a ravishing smile and murmuring, "I've heard *so* much about you, Mr. Savage."

She seemed surprised and a trifle disappointed when the bronze man was not overwhelmed. If he was affected at all, the symptoms failed to register visibly.

"She came west when she heard her father was—had passed away," Sagebrush Smith explained.

The bronze man nodded slightly, and turned over a newspaper bearing headlines about the discovery of the "spirit radio" to show that he already had the information.

Ham pointed at the headlines. "You've read about the machine, Doc? It's an incredible thing, isn't it?"

"Yes."

"It's plumb goofy if you ask me," interposed Sagebrush Smith. "There ain't no such thing as spirits."

Doc Savage's strange flake gold eyes rested on the cowboy with inscrutable intentness. "What do you think will happen to you after death?" the bronze man asked.

"Why, I—uh——" Sagebrush swallowed. "How the blazes would I know?"

"The belief in life hereafter is too general, too firmly established, to be ignored," the bronze man said. "Our Christians believe in Heaven, the Buddhists believe in Nirvana, the Mohammedans in *Falak al afla,* and even the American Indian had his Happy Hunting Ground. From time immemorial, all races, creeds, and stages of civilized beings have believed in life after death."

The bronze man paused, and silence had the effect of driving home what his powerful voice had just stated.

"No belief of mankind has stood the test of ages with unshaken strength as this one has," he continued. "And it is not enough to pass the phenomena off by saying that man, wishing to live forever, conjures up belief in everlasting life to mentally console himself. It is more profound than that. It is deeper. The utter foundation of all religions.

"Certainly we know that the Christian religion, for instance, is based on actuality. Nor has any scientist ever proven, for example, that one word of the Scriptural Bible is false. Hence, in the face of such overwhelming evidence, we who are here in this room are hardly justified in saying there cannot be existence in some medium after death."

Sagebrush Smith rubbed his jaw. "What I meant to say was that the static you hear on your radio is caused by lightnin'."

"Only part of it," Doc Savage said. "When a lightning flash comes, you hear a burst of static on your radio. But there are many forms of static noises on a radio—atmospheric lightning, frictional static, earth currents. There are, too, forms of static for which science has never been able to define sources, and such static is present in the remotest desert, in the middle of the largest ocean, and has been heard at the north and south poles."

He paused. "One thing," he said seriously, "is most mysterious about static."

"What's that?" asked the cowboy.

"Science," Doc Savage said, *"has never succeeded in eliminating static from radio reception."*

"Say," grunted Sagebrush, "that's right."

"Radio static," the bronze man said, "has been one of the most elusive and mysterious things science has ever tried to fathom."

Sagebrush Smith swallowed several times. Then he pointed at the vault-steel box of Meander Surett.

"You mean," he gulped, "that the machine there really translates static into messages from people who are dead?"

Doc Savage shook his head.

"No," he said quietly. "The device is worthless."

THE listeners stood in a shocked silence; they felt suspended, hanging in space. Their excitement had climbed up a ladder of belief that the machine of Meander Surett could talk with spirits, and now suddenly the ladder was nothing. They couldn't find words.

The blond girl was first to speak.

"How do you know?" she demanded.

"The result of examination," the bronze man explained.

It was evident that he had made an examination. Meander Surett's vault-steel box stood open on the table, and the cover panels of insulating material had been removed from the device therein to disclose wiring, tubes, coils, intricate gears and tiny motors, a moving roll of photosensitized tape, a tiny pin-beam of fluctuating light after the nature of telephoto devices, and more, much more, that even Monk, who was versed in electrochemistry, could not identify.

The girl seemed impatiently unconvinced.

"My father worked a lifetime on that," she said sharply. "You examine it for a few minutes——"

"For almost four hours," the bronze man corrected.

"For four hours then! How can you tell in such a short time that it won't work?"

Before he answered, the bronze man picked up a thick sheaf of blueprints and typewritten explanatory matter enclosed in a neat binder labeled:

CONSTRUCTION DATA OF STATIC TRANSLATOR
BY MEANDER SURETT

"This was in the steel case," Doc said. "The explanation it gives is detailed, and the construction of the device follows identically the blueprints. However"—he tossed the binder of papers into the vault-steel box—"the contrivance is based on an utterly unworkable electrical theory. It cannot possibly function."

The blond girl nipped her lips with white teeth.

"But——"

"I am sorry," the bronze man said. "However, it is better that you know the truth—at once, and that the public know, as well. I have telephoned the newspapers that the device is unworkable."

"You've what?" the girl screamed.

"Advised the newspapers and press associations that Meander Surett's invention will not work," Doc Savage said.

The girl glared.

"You had no right to do that!"

Doc Savage did not reply.

"You might have waited!" the girl cried.

"For what?" the bronze man asked.

The blond young woman stamped a foot. "I don't like what you've done!" she shrieked. "I don't see why my father was crazy enough to get you mixed up in this! I don't believe this machine is worthless! I think you're lying!"

The fact that the bronze man showed no emotion did not surprise Monk and Ham, who knew the remarkable control which he could exercise over his facial expression.

"You have the privilege," Doc said slowly, "of believing whatever you wish."

"I don't trust you!" the girl repeated. "I'm going to take that machine and walk out of here with it."

"What," Doc inquired, "do you plan to do with it?"

"That's my private business!" said the young woman. "But for your information, I'm going to hire a *real* expert to examine the device. And if you try to stop me, I'll call the police!"

The bronze man made a slight gesture. "You are welcome to it. Either myself or one of my colleagues will carry it to a taxicab for you."

The girl pointed at Sagebrush Smith. "I'd rather he carried it," she said coldly.

Sagebrush Smith, looking somewhat confused, went grunting and stumbling outside with the box. The girl followed him.

Doc Savage walked over and closed the door after them. Then the bronze man glanced at Monk and Ham.

"You two had better stick here in this room," he said. "It may be dangerous to get out until we learn what is behind this."

"But ain't it all over?" Monk gulped.

"Hardly," Doc said. "In my opinion, it has only started."

"Whatcha mean, Doc?"

Instead of answering, the bronze man opened the window. He produced from inside his clothing a small collapsible grapple of alloy steel to which was attached a thin, extremely stout, silken cord of a length to more than reach the ground.

"Long Tom, Johnny, and Renny have been working on this thing in New York," he said.

Monk and Ham were surprised. The three men Doc named were: Major Thomas J. "Long Tom" Roberts, the electrical wizard; William Harper "Johnny" Littlejohn, the geologist and archæologist, and Colonel John "Renny" Renwick, the engineer. The trio were the remaining members of Doc Savage's coteries of assistants. It had been the opinion of Monk and Ham up to now that the matter of Meander Surett's letter was not serious enough for Doc Savage to put all his men to work on it.

"You mean that Long Tom, Johnny and Renny learned something important?" Monk demanded.

Doc Savage nodded.

"They learned that a man named Everett Everett Barr, an ex-carnival swindler and now a shyster lawyer, formerly employed Sally Surett in his office."

"But what has that to do——"

"Everett Everett Barr," Doc Savage said, "had the confidence of Sally Surett. She did not know he was a crook. She showed him letters from her father, and asked Barr how to find Meander Surett. She wanted to hire detectives to find her father, because she was worried about his long disappearance."

"That's natural," Monk admitted.

"Everett Everett Barr evidently learned of this 'static translator' from Meander Surett's letters to his daughter," the bronze man said. "I am merely surmising that. But Johnny, Long Tom, and Renny did learn that Barr became much interested and sent a man named Bill Horder to Death Valley to find Meander Surett and kill him.

"Bill Horder poisoned Meander Surett in such a fashion that Surett thought he had internal cancer. But Meander Surett also caught Horder prowling around the desert laboratory and killed him. That left Everett Everett Barr up in the air with his plot, because he had no idea where Meander Surett's laboratory was located. No idea, that is, until he read that the old scientist was found dead. Barr at once hired the Lazy Y cowboys to get the steel box. And Barr himself has come from New York by plane."

"But what is this Everett Everett Barr's plot?" Monk demanded.

"That," Doc Savage said, "is one of *two* things we must learn."

"Two things?"

"The second thing," Doc Savage explained, "is the whereabouts of Sally Surett."

"But Sally Surett just left here with the box!" Monk exclaimed. "The blond girl——"

"The blond girl is not Sally Surett."

"Not——"

"However," Doc Savage added, "she does answer the description of Everett Everett Barr's wife."

THE bronze man swung out the window and slid down to the street. Monk and Ham, peering out the window, watched him vanish in the shrubbery which edged the street.

A few moments later, Sagebrush Smith and the bogus Sally Surett came out of the hotel with the box.

Monk drew back from the window, took out a handkerchief and wiped his homely face.

"Whew!" he said.

"Maybe you'll learn that you can't judge women, you freak of nature," Ham said. "You thought that blonde was on the level."

"You didn't, of course?"

"I thought," Ham said dryly, "there was something phony about her."

"That lie should make you black in the face!" Monk growled.

The two associates contemplated each other in sour silence. Their pets, Habeas and Chemistry, apparently partaking of the mood of their owners, sat down in the middle of the hotel room and showed each other their teeth.

"You know," Monk said, "you can't never tell about Doc."

"What do you mean, tree-dweller?"

"You go along and you think you know what Doc is doing," Monk explained. "And then, whango! You find out he's got hold of a rope when you thought he only had a string."

"If it wasn't against my policy to agree with you," Ham admitted, "I'd say you were right."

Chapter X

BRONZE SHADOW

Doc Savage had prepared from childhood for the unusual career which he was to follow. He was a product of careful, modern thinking, an example of what the most absolute possible training can do for the human body and mind.

His major training had been in science, because science is the future enemy of organized and individual crime, as police departments of the world have come to realize in the last decade.

In keeping with his reliance on scientific methods, the bronze man had developed, and was continually developing, unusual devices, gadgets which he employed in unexpected fashions. He kept as many of them with him as possible, wearing for this purpose a pocket-vest designed and padded so as to be as inconspicuous as was feasible.

Doc Savage, having quitted the hotel room by the only method which would have enabled him to reach the street unobserved ahead of Sagebrush Smith and the fake Sally Surett, faded into the concealment of shrubbery. He moved a few yards, at the same time withdrawing two packages from a special pocket inside his coat.

One of the packages was wrapped with plain tough brown grocery paper and was near the proportions of a fifty-size box of cigars.

The other package was not wrapped; it was, more properly, a leather case.

The Surfside was large enough to have a telegraph office in the same building. Doc Savage entered this with his packages.

Sagebrush Smith and the blond girl were putting the metal box into a taxicab when a telegraph messenger boy hurried up and handed the cab driver Doc's package which was wrapped in brown paper. The messenger also presented a five-dollar bill.

"After you have taken these passengers wherever they want to go," said the messenger, "deliver this package to the home of the manager of this hotel." He gave the manager's home address. "The five dollars is for your trouble," he added.

"Gosh, sure!" said the taxi driver.

About that time, in the hotel, Doc Savage was speaking to the hotel manager. "Later in the night a package will be delivered to your home," the bronze man said. "Just return it to me, if you will."

"Of course, Mr. Savage," said the manager.

The taxicab driver got behind the wheel with his package. Sagebrush Smith and the girl got in the back with their box. The girl gave an address, and the cab moved.

When the cab was out of sight, Doc Savage came out of the hotel; entered another taxicab, settled back on the cushions, and opened his leather case. He telescoped up a small directional loop antenna, donned a headset, and tuned in the miniature short-wave radio transmitter which was in the package carried by the driver of the blonde girl's taxicab. The directional radio showed that the other cab had turned sharply to the right and was heading for the part of town where traffic was thickest.

After that the directional radio gadget enabled the bronze man to trail his quarry while he himself followed entirely different streets.

THE blonde girl, when her cab was in very thick traffic, leaned forward and tapped the window to get the driver's attention. She asked to be taken to a different address. Ten minutes later, she did the same thing again. All the while, she watched the rear window, intensely interested in their back trail throughout the ride.

Sagebrush Smith commented on this.

"Doc Savage," the girl explained, "may try to follow us. I'm just making sure he doesn't."

Finally, she gave the address of a midtown hotel which was not too particular about its guests. The cab pulled up before this hostelry. The hotel boasted no doorman. The two bell boys were runts who strained vainly with the Meander Surett steel chest.

A very large hump-shouldered colored man approached. He walked with a limp.

"Ah carry dat foah two bits," he offered.

"You need two bits worse than we need the exercise," said Sagebrush Smith. "You're hired."

The way the confidence of the colored fellow evaporated when he took hold of the chest made Sagebrush Smith grin. However, the big darky stuck to the bargain and staggered into the hotel with the chest. There was no elevator. He shuffled up the steps, seeming to have a great deal of difficulty, although, somewhat strangely, he was not perspiring at all when he reached the top.

The blonde girl knocked on a door.

The man who opened the door liked trinkets. His cigarette was stuck in a long holder, and the cigarette was monogrammed "E.E.B." His nose-pincher spectacles had a flowing black ribbon. He wore a béret emblazoned with a yachtsman's gold-braided insignia.

His free hand held an elaborate patent lighter. His wrist watch had hands and faces to register second, minute, hour, day, month, year, and the temperature. A patent pedometer was strapped around his other wrist. An array consisting of a pencil-flashlight, a two-colors-of-ink fountain pen and a fountain-pen-tear-gas-gun stuck in his vest pocket.

Otherwise he was a round, well-fed man with twinkling devil eyes and lips which were always making shapes. His clothing was expensive and about as loud as it could be without causing people to follow him down streets.

"Well, well," he said. "Well, well, well, I do declare!"

"This"—the blonde girl indicated Sagebrush—"is Sagebrush Smith."

The round man dropped his cigarette holder. He picked it up again quickly.

"I'm delighted," he said heartily, "really and truly delighted to meet you, because any friend of Miss Surett's is a friend of mine and a very dear friend, too."

"Howdy," said Sagebrush bluntly. "What's your name?"

The round man busied himself taking short puffs of his cigarette until he caught a slight nod from the blonde girl.

"I am Everett Everett Barr, attorney at law," the round man then explained. "Yes, sir, attorney at law, and a friend to Miss Surett, as well as one who feels just as though Miss Surett was his own daughter."

"Mr. Barr," the girl explained, "came out by plane to see that I got the full benefits of my father's great discovery."

"Yes, indeed." Mr. Barr made a clucking noise of disapproval. "Unfortunately, there are men who will take advantage of a young girl. Ah—some men who are quite famous stoop to such scoundrelly tactics, I am sorry to say."

He caught a glimpse of the big darky with the chest.

"My goodness!" exclaimed Mr. Barr. "Do bring that right in, Rastus, my boy, my good fellow."

The black man shuffled in and deposited the chest on the floor.

"Here's your two bits," said Sagebrush.

"Yes, yes, and here's fifty cents more for your trouble," volunteered Mr. Barr generously.

The black man took the coins and shuffled out.

EVERETT EVERETT BARR was full of enthusiasm; he was so stuffed with delight that he could not restrain himself. He bounced over, seized Sagebrush Smith's hand and gave it another hearty pumping.

"Young man, you seem like a wonderful, upstanding, wide-awake and clean-limbed fellow," he declared. "A true son of the West."

Sagebrush grew uncomfortable. "Doc Savage claims that contraption in the box ain't worth a hoot," he muttered.

"*Tsk, tsk,*" clucked Mr. Barr. "An unfortunate error, I do fear."

Sagebrush frowned. "Doc Savage," he said, "has got a reputation."

"But I do hope you haven't taken him too literally, my young friend?"

"He kinda impressed me," Sagebrush said.

Everett Everett Barr sighed regretfully. "Youth is always so impressionable," he murmured.

At this point, there was a knock on the door.

It was the big colored man again.

"Ah done drop mah rabbit's foot in dis heah room," he explained sheepishly.

"Why, I do declare," said Mr. Barr. He looked around. "Well, you certainly did drop it because there it is."

Every one looked at the rabbit foot, a natural thing to do—every one except the colored gentleman, who seized the diversion to stoop, open a slit in the carpet with a razor-sharp pocket-knife and slipped a flat metal plaque through the slit.

"Ah sho done thank yo-all," he mumbled as he received back his rabbit foot.

The large darky withdrew from the room, closing the door, and backed carefully down the hall—stringing a hair-fine wire which ran from the plaque, sticking it against the wall with unnoticeable bits of transparent wax called "magnetite," stuff magicians use to cause things to stick to their fingers. Entering a near-by room which he had just rented, the darky connected a powerful amplifier to the almost invisible wire.

The black man then became Doc Savage by removing his dark, curly wig. He donned a telephonic headset and listened to what was being picked up by the velocity microphone which he had planted under the carpet.

Everett Everett Barr was saying, "Miss Surett, my dear girl, have you had dinner?"

"No," the blonde admitted.

"You two children run along and eat," ordered Mr. Barr. "You'll enjoy Miss Surett's company, I'm sure you will, Mr. Sagebrush Smith."

"I sure will!" agreed Sagebrush enthusiastically.

"Take your time," requested Mr. Barr. "Yes, indeed. Take plenty of time, because I shall be entertaining visitors in a private conference while you are out. Ah—you might telephone and see if I am at liberty before you return."

There was the sound of a door opening and closing, and after that, silence, so evidently Sagebrush Smith and the fake Sally Surett had gone out to eat.

A FEW minutes later, Mr. Barr removed the telephone receiver and asked for a number.

"You can come up now, Hoke, my pal, my friend," he said.

It took about five minutes for Hoke McGee and his Lazy Y cowboys to arrive in answer to the summons.

As they came in the door, Mr. Barr made one very loud and emphatic remark.

"Phew!" he said.

"Now don't start that!" Hoke McGee snarled. "People have been goin' *phew!* at us until we're danged good and tired of it!"

Mr. Barr made his clucking noise. "Goodness!" he said. "Gracious, what an—er—— By any chance, have you been trapping, raising, or otherwise associating with the *mephitis mephitis?*"

Hoke scowled. "What's that?"

"The lowly skunk," said Mr. Barr.

Hoke McGee swore for one half a minute without once repeating himself.

"We ain't in the mood for funny stuff!" he yelled. "It ain't funny, anyway! It's danged serious!"

"What do you mean?"

"We're victims!" Hoke shouted. "We've had the lowest trick pulled on us that could be pulled!"

"By whom, may I ask?" inquired Mr. Barr.

"By Doc Savage."

Judging from the nervous quality in Everett Everett Barr's cough, mention of Doc Savage did not have a soothing effect on his nerves.

"Er—what happened?" he asked anxiously.

"We had a disinfection inspection as the train came into Los Angeles county!" Hoke gritted.

"There is no such thing," said Barr, "as a disinfection inspection."

"We know that now!" Hoke swore some more. "We've got it figured out that the big white-headed hombre who pulled the disinfection inspection gag was Doc Savage or one of his outfit. He made us peel our shirts and rubbed us with somethin' out of a bottle."

"And what," inquired Mr. Barr, "happened then?"

"Can't you smell?"

"You mean *that* has happened to you?"

"Sure!" Hoke McGee swore some more.

"Why not take baths?" inquired Mr. Barr.

"We did, dang-blast it—and it only made us smell worse! That stuff he put on us was a chemical or somethin'." The Lazy Y foreman fell into a chair and held his own nose. "You got no idea how it is to be like this. Why, dogs run barkin' after us for blocks. They won't let us ride the street cars. We got throwed outta our hotel."

"This seems most amazing!" murmured Everett Everett Barr.

"It's the dangest-fool thing I ever heard of!" Hoke snarled. The Lazy Y foreman smashed his fists on the chair arms and ground his teeth. "He could 'a' shot us, poisoned us, or had us arrested, and it wouldn't 'a' been this serious. Do you realize what it means if we can't get this stuff off us?"

"Why—er—you will become social outcasts," Mr. Barr admitted.

Hoke McGee got up from the chair. He put out his jaw.

"It means," he gritted, "that we're gonna have a hot time gettin' hold of that box!"

"Hoke, my—ah—aromatic acquaintance," said Mr. Barr, "you needn't worry further about the vault-steel chest. I have it." He arose and opened the door of a closet into which the metal case had been inserted. "I have it, as you can see," he repeated delightedly.

Hoke McGee made an audible noise as he swallowed.

"What about the twenty-five thousand dollars we was to get?" he gulped.

"Don't be ridiculous, my good friend," said Mr. Barr.

THIS time, Hoke McGee swore for three full minutes without once repeating himself. He ended up by shouting, "Welcher! Welcher! Welcher!" at the top of his voice.

"Hoke, you wrong me," declared Everett Everett Barr in an injured tone. "I do not intend to pay for work which you did not do. You were to get the case. You did not. It was recovered for me by my good and valued helpmate—I mean, by a young lady, who, even if I do say so, is an accomplished actress."

"You ain't lost your carnival grifter ways! You're gonna freeze us out! Well, you won't!"

"And what," asked Mr. Barr, "will stop me?"

At this point Hoke McGee evidently came over and gave Mr. Barr a hard shove which deposited him forcibly in a chair, because the Barr grunt was loud and surprised.

"You cut us in on this, whatever it is," said Hoke menacingly, "or we go to the cops and explain how you hired an hombre named Bill Horder to kill old Meander Surett."

Everett Everett Barr made a strangling noise.

"Hoke, you wouldn't do that!"

"Wouldn't I!"

"But, Hoke, my colleague, my old pard, my good——"

"Nuts!" said Hoke. "Bushels of nuts, all with worms in 'em!"

There was silence for a time, during which Mr. Barr evidently considered alternatives. So sensitive was the microphone-and-amplifier eavesdropping arrangement which Doc Savage was using that the breathing of the men in the room was clearly audible, along with the excited ticking of several watches, probably of the large variety commonly carried by cowboys and called "turnips."

"Goodness!" said Mr. Barr plaintively. "I—ah—well, it seems I have no choice."

"Now you're talkin' sense," Hoke said. "And we'll be fair about it. The Lazy Y fell down so far, we admit. But we'll go along with you from now on, and when this is over, we get the twenty-five grand. How's that?"

"Not"—Mr. Barr seemed sad—"exactly what I would have wished for. But I will agree."

"That's great," Hoke said.

"However," said Everett Everett Barr wildly, "you must keep out of smelling distance. I—ah—cannot have you around here. You are not exactly bouquets, you know."

"That's all right," Hoke said gloomily. "We'll go out and see if we can find a hotel that will take in hombres smellin' like we do."

"Er—be careful about any more disinfection inspectors," said Mr. Barr dryly.

Hoke McGee was saying things as he stamped out.

Chapter XI

THE PUBLICITY BOX

WHEN Sagebrush Smith and the bogus Sally Surett returned to the hotel room, Everett Everett Barr greeted them heartily.

"Good evening, good evening," he said. "You two make a charming couple, you really do. Won't you sit down until the gentlemen of the press arrive?"

"Gentlemen of the press?" said Sagebrush vacantly.

"Newspaper reporters," explained Mr. Barr.

"But what's a newspaper reporter comin' here for?" Sagebrush wanted to know.

Everett Everett Barr now gave evidence of considerable seriousness. He arose and paced twice around the hotel room, hands clasped behind his back, after which he struck a dramatic pose, one thumb hooked into the pocket which held his pencil-flashlight, fountain-pen-tear-gas-gun and two-colors-of-ink fountain pen; and his other hand, the one with the wrist that wore the pedometer, leveled rigidly at a stack of newspapers bearing headlines saying that Doc Savage had declared Meander Surett's invention worthless.

"Doc Savage," he announced, "has committed a dastardly offense."

"Dastardly offense?"

"This Savage," said Barr, "has given out a statement to the newspapers declaring flatly that the great invention of

Meander Surett is no invention at all. Fraudulently, without warrant, right or permission, actual or implied, he made a statement of such nature to the press, and in so proceeding he committed fraud, libel and misrepresentation, all monetarily and spiritually injurious to my client."

"Your client?"

"This darling little girl, Miss Sally Surett, is my client," Mr. Barr explained.

Newspapermen began arriving before Sagebrush Smith could inquire what measures Mr. Barr intended to take against Doc Savage, as well as offer a personal opinion that the best thing for any one to do was to leave Doc Savage alone.

The gentlemen of the press impressed Sagebrush Smith as being a baggy-kneed lot. They showed more initial interest in some bottles of champagne which Everett Everett Barr produced for their consumption. The representatives of the Fourth Estate were in need of shaves and the attentions of a suit-pressing establishment.

There were big reporters, little reporters, fat ones and thin ones, and one slender fellow who seemed to be an Italian. The latter carried an umbrella and wore rubbers, although there was not a cloud in the California sky.

"Sheeza maybe rain an' I be fix," the reportorial Latin explained gloomily.

AFTER corks popped and champagne fizzed, Everett Everett Barr got down to brass tacks and began explaining that the great scientist, Meander Surett, had made an invention before his death, and that Doc Savage had declared the discovery to be worthless. Mr. Barr crashed his fist against the table with great force.

"Gentlemen!" he shouted. "Doc Savage was wrong! He is a great man possibly, but he is utterly wrong! *The invention of Meander Surett will work!*"

A reporter picked up a champagne bottle and looked at it. "Nothing wrong with your champagne," he said. "But as for your ideas—well, if Doc Savage says the thing won't work, it won't work, as far as I am concerned."

"Young man," said Mr. Barr, "you are impressed by a reputation!"

The reporter shrugged. "Then so are most of the great

scientists in the world, and every crook who has heard of Doc Savage," he said.

The remark gave Mr. Barr something that looked a trifle like indigestion.

"Ah—well—ahem——" He cleared his throat. "We might drop that line of discussion," he said. "It is of no importance in ascertaining whether or not Meander Surett's device will work."

"It seems to me to be doggone important," the reporter persisted. "Doc Savage says it won't work, and his opinion carries weight."

Mr. Barr shook his head.

"No," he said. "Doc Savage did not have all the device!"

"Eh?"

"One important attachment was missing," Mr. Barr explained.

The reporters were interested.

"Did Doc Savage know that he wasn't examining all the machine?" one demanded.

"No," Mr. Barr said. "Savage did not know that."

"Where is the missing part?"

"Meander Surett's daughter, Sally, has it," replied Everett Everett Barr. "My old friend Meander Surett was not without acumen, gentlemen, and he did not trust this man, Savage, fully, so he removed one very essential item from his device, installed it in a separate case and sent it to his daughter, making no mention of the fact to Doc Savage."

"You mean," a newspaperman demanded, "that you can stick this part in the contraption, and it will work in spite of what Savage said?"

"We hope so," Mr. Barr said seriously.

"'How about giving a demonstration?"

"That is why you gentlemen were summoned here."

EVERETT EVERETT BARR went to a closet and secured a stout leather bag which he handed to the blonde girl with an impressive gesture. The girl, with impressive solemnity, removed a key from the end of the stout silk ribbon which was around her neck and used this to unlock the bag, then lifted out a crackle-finished metal case of the type used to enclose amplifiers in public-address systems. A cable containing several wires, each carefully labeled, ran from this.

Everett Everett Barr produced a paper and said, "Here are directions for connecting the attachment, supplied by Meander Surett." He worked with a screw driver and a pair of pliers for some minutes, hooking the new device onto the large one in the steel chest.

"I betta two to one she's notta work," said the Italian journalist.

The other scribes only grinned derisively at him.

"Ten to one she's notta work," the Italian offered.

None of the reporters had faith enough in the machine to take him up.

Everett Everett Barr finished attaching the auxiliary device. He turned various switches while carefully consulting the directions supplied by Meander Surett.

"Gentlemen," he said smilingly, "you understand that I am not a technical expert, and hence I cannot explain exactly how the device operates. But even if I were a technical expert, I should not reveal the nature of Meander Surett's discovery, for that would be violating the best interests of the famous inventor's bereaved daughter"—he paused to pat the blonde's shoulder—"who is here to witness the test of her father's incredible static-translator."

A faint whirring came from the machine, accompanied by a sporadic clicking sound such as stock tickers make.

"Must be da spook rappa in da thing," offered the Italian.

Everett Everett Barr frowned.

"This is scientific and practical." He looked around. "My dear friends, I will tell you what Meander Surett wrote his dear daughter about the theory of his discovery. He said that science has long known that all matter is composed of electricity—positive and negative electrons, or conceivably some smaller division which science has not yet discovered.

"It was the theory of Meander Surett that everything is electricity. *Everything!* Therefore the immortal, the everlasting part of the human being—and I mean, of course, the spirit—would have to be electricity, too. The spirit therefore could conceivably react on sensitive electrical apparatus.

"It could convey a message, you understand, just as you and I step up and speak into a telephone, or as a telegraph operator taps a telegraph key, providing we living humans could create a device which the spirits of the departed could actuate.

"Meander Surett accomplished this by arranging a moving light beam which may be shifted in different directions by the electrical vibrations in the infra-short wave lengths of radio."

"Sheeza get kinda complicated," suggested the Latin.

"Indeed it is," Mr. Barr agreed. "I will make it simple. I will say that Meander Surett merely created a highly complicated scientific pencil with which astral beings may write messages."

"To make this really good," a tabloid man chuckled, "somebody oughta go in a trance."

Mr. Barr took out his handerchief and wiped his forehead.

"I do wish," he complained, "that this operation did not approach so closely the discredited methods of so-called mind readers and mediums. I fear you do not realize how important this is."

The machine continued to purr and make clicking noises.

"When does a message come out?" a man demanded.

"Patience," Mr. Barr requested. "The message is written with a tiny beam of light which moves over a sensitized photographic paper after the fashion of our modern telephoto machines."

They waited about ten minutes before a line of tape began to creep from the machine. Mr. Barr appeared hardly able to restrain himself until the first sentence was completed. He tore off the tape and stared at it.

"Jehoshaphat!" he cried.

He gazed around at the newspapermen, profound astonishment on his round face.

"Meander Surett was murdered!" he shouted.

There was shocked silence.

"A man named Bill Horder killed poor Meander Surett with poison!" Mr. Barr yelled.

DURING ensuing seconds, the state of the room was best described as silent confusion. The newspapermen were astounded, speechless. If this was true, it would be one of the biggest news breaks of all time!

"Is that tape—is it a message from—Meander Surett?" a man croaked.

Everett Everett Barr nodded solemnly. "It appears to be a communication from the great scientist," he said. He passed the strip of photographic paper to the blonde girl. "Is this your father's handwriting?" he asked gravely.

The blonde took one glance at the jittery white line registered on the paper. She burst into tears.

"It's dad's—writing," she said between sobs.

Silently, Everett Everett Barr passed the portentous strip of photographic paper around for examination. The newshawks read:

> *My desire to be first. . . . Meander Surett. . . . I am quite happy here beyond. . . . I was murdered by a man named Bill Horder. . . . Poison. . . . Seemed to be cancer. . . . I killed Horder and buried him one hundred yards west of my laboratory.*

While this was being read, all were aware that the device was purring and clicking again.

"Another message is coming!" Everett Everett Barr announced solemnly.

Several newspapermen had made movements toward the door, but now they restrained themselves.

Mr. Barr tore off the next message and examined it.

"This," he said hollowly, "seems to be a communication from a man named Harold A. Beaver. I confess that the fellow is a complete stranger to me."

A journalist tried to speak twice and finally had to cough to get his words loose.

"Harold A. Beaver was murdered here in Los Angeles about a year ago," he muttered. "Shot to death. They sent his widow to the penitentiary for killing him after they found a twenty-thousand-dollar insurance policy on his life—drawn in her favor. The policy was hidden. Widow claimed she hadn't known there was a policy at all. They made the jury believe she'd killed her husband, then gotten scared and hid the policy."

Everett Everett Barr seemed so astonished at this that he could not stay on his feet. He collapsed into a chair.

"Gentlemen!" he gasped. "Gentlemen, this invention of Meander Surett's means there will never be another murder upon this earth! Read what the spirit of Harold A. Beaver writes. Then you'll understand!"

The newsmen read:

This is Harold A. Beaver. . . . My wife is innocent. . . . I was killed by my business partner. . . . I was the only one who knew he had robbed our firm. . . . He buried the murder gun under his garage floor. . . . Insurance agent will identify him as man who took out policy on my life to throw blame on my wife.

Every newspaperman reacted to this instantaneously and in the same fashion—by making a wild rush for the nearest telephone.

The Italian charged out of the room after the others, but instead of leaving the hotel, he ran down the corridor and entered the room in which Doc Savage was eavesdropping with a telephone headset over his ears.

Monk, who was crouched astraddle a chair and also wearing a headset, looked up. His homely face was incredulous.

"Blazes!" he muttered. "I didn't expect anythin' like this to happen!"

Doc Savage and Monk listened while Ham removed his Italian disguise and at the same time explained exactly what had happened in the other room and described the additional attachment which Everett Everett Barr had connected to old Meander Surett's invention.

"Doc," Ham finished, "do you think it possible that the extra gadget could have made the contrivance work?"

There was a long silence—a silence of sufficient length that Monk and Ham saw that the bronze man was not going to commit himself on the point.

"Doc," Monk muttered, "are you even sure that blonde girl in there isn't the real Sally Surett?"

The bronze man was silent for some time.

Then he said, "Renny, Long Tom and Johnny, investigating in New York, forwarded a detailed description of Sally Surett, which they secured by making inquiries at her rooming house and around Everett Everett Barr's office. They also managed to get a picture." He produced a photographic print. "They had it telephotoed out here."

He handed the picture to Monk and Ham. "This is Sally Surett. Does it even resemble that blonde girl?"

Monk and Ham examined a photograph of a small, dark-haired and very pretty young woman with a nice face who certainly had no resemblance to the blonde.

"I don't savvy this," Monk muttered. "Did you hear what he got out of that machine? The truth! The fact that Bill Horder murdered Meander Surett!"

Ham nodded. For once, he seemed too preoccupied to disagree with Monk.

"I could hardly believe my eyes when I read the tape," the lawyer muttered. "Barr would be the last man in the world to want that to get out."

"Did you watch Barr's face at the time?" Doc Savage inquired.

"He looked plenty upset," Ham said.

Doc Savage put the headset down. "Barr, the girl and Sagebrush Smith have gone to see the police about the message from Harold Beaver," he said.

The bronze man remained motionless for some time, his metallic features inscrutable. Then, so low at first that it was almost unnoticeable, the trilling note came into being, rising and falling, musical and exotic—the small, fantastic thing which the man of bronze did unconsciously in moments of mental stress—of surprise or puzzlement.

"We will watch Barr," he said. "It is only a question of time until we learn what he is planning, or get a clue to the whereabouts of the real Sally Surett."

Chapter XII

CAPTAIN SCUTTLE

THE police found the revolver under the garage floor of the late Harold Beaver's business partner. They took the partner to the insurance agent, and he was identified as the man who had taken out an insurance policy on Harold Beaver's life in the name of Beaver's wife. The partner was arrested.

The district attorney announced that Mrs. Harold Beaver would be released from the women's penitentiary as soon as it could possibly be arranged.

The newspapers went wild. They got out their biggest type. One newspaper covered its front page with enormous headlines and explained in a boxed item on the editorial page that:

> "We think this story of Meander Surett's invention so amazing that we are using the special batch of type which we were saving for the Second Coming of Christ."

An expedition went into Death Valley by plane, exhumed Meander Surett's body and performed an autopsy, learning that the man had died of an acid poisoning with symptoms probably similar to that of cancer.

It was remarked that some one had apparently already conducted an investigation. The body of Bill Horder was found buried where the "Static Translator" message of Meander Surett had said they would find it buried.

So everything had checked out to prove the message from the device to be a genuine one.

Human nature is consistent. School kids like to catch their teacher in a mistake, and every employee likes to show up his boss as being wrong; nothing tickles an average individual like seeing a highly touted expert stub his toe, and be proven wrong.

The fact that Doc Savage was a highly touted expert was not of his own choosing. The bronze man disapproved of publicity because it gave enemies too much of a line on him, and because he was fundamentally not an exhibitionist.

Doc Savage was not surprised when the newspapers insisted with great enthusiasm that he had been utterly wrong about Meander Surett's invention. It was not the first time the daily journals had opposed the bronze man; some newspapers resented the fact that Doc ordinarily did not give out interviews.

The bronze man's reticence was doubly aggravating because his doings were front-page news. By way of getting revenge, the papers welcomed chances to knock the bronze man with editorials.

"They're gonna caw at us like crows after an owl," Monk complained.

"The best thing we can do," Doc Savage explained, "is disappear for a while."

"Disappear?"

"As far as public notice is concerned."

"What about the rest of our gang in New York—Renny, Long Tom and Johnny?" Monk asked.

"They will remain in New York for the time," Doc decided. "Action of this thing many shift back to New York, and, too, they are busy back there, hunting some trace of the genuine Sally Surett."

Hence when a flock of reporters and cameramen descended upon the Hotel Surfside, it was found that Doc Savage and his men had vanished.

That same day, a new taxicab took up a stand in front of the grimy little hostelry frequented by Everett Everett Barr, fake Sally Surett and Sagebrush Smith.

The driver of this hack was a squat Mexican who wore

a large hat habitually yanked down over his eyes, colored glasses, and who sported an item not every Mexican possessed—a beard. A close acquaintance would have had to inspect the cab driver closely to recognize Monk.

Ham, disguised as the wiry Latin journalist, continued to appear in every conference which Everett Everett Barr held with the press. He possessed credentials saying he represented a paper owned by Premier Mussolini of Italy, and no one suspected otherwise.

Doc Savage returned to his disguise of a large colored man, and acquired a job as cleaning-man around Everett Everett Barr's hotel.

Habeas and Chemistry were left in a rooming house near Barr's hotel that Doc had rented for his own use.

THERE were developments.

Sally Surett began to receive monetary offers for the invention of her father, these ranging up to one of a million dollars outright. And all the offers, of course, were contingent upon it being proven beyond shadow of doubt that the device was what it portended to be. And Everett Everett Barr turned down all propositions in the name of Sally Surett.

SURETT DISCOVERY NOT TO BE SOLD
TO BE GIVEN TO BENEFIT MANKIND

This was what the headlines said. The story quoted Mr. Barr as saying in press conference:

> "Realizing fully that this is no ordinary invention, but one which will have a sweeping effect on the character of the world's inhabitants, my client, Miss Sally Surett, is not going to demand one penny for the invention, but will give it outright to benefit mankind.
>
> "Just exactly how it will be given, however, is something that we have not yet decided; and in the meantime, we are going to operate the machine once daily, and representatives of the public, meaning the newspapermen, will be admitted."

Ham reported this announcement to Doc Savage.

"I still don't see," Ham complained, "what that shyster is up to. Still, I'm as sure as can be that he's a crook."

The homely Monk grinned.

"They say it takes a crook to recognize a crook," he chuckled. "In this case, it's a shyster lawyer to recognize another shyster."

"You hairy numskull," Ham snapped, "I'm behind on keeping you in line!"

"You talk to me in that tone," Monk said, "and I'll tap you one on that knot you call a head and you'll be untying your shoe strings under the impression they're neckties."

THE commotion over Meander Surett's machine was not long in coming. Like snowballs and wars, it started small and grew.

It began with the demand of a spectacular, noisy, flamboyant and notorious female evangelist that the "Static Translator" be destroyed as an instrument of the devil. It was a sin, said the evangelist, to have communication with the departed.

Just why it was a sin was something the evangelist neglected to explain, but the newspapermen thought that if there was any sin, it might be the way the evangelist snatched at everything that came along to get personal notoriety.

But the real cannon roar from this incident came when the "Translator" clicked out a message from a departed uncle of the evangelist, the uncle explaining that he could testify from personal experience that there was a Purgatory, and for the evangelist in the future to give more attention to the Holy Bible and less to personal gain, or there would be another of the family down there. The newspaper-reading world got a hearty chuckle out of that.

The "Static Translator" thereafter developed into "a confession box for spooks," as one periodical dubbed it.

A banker, whose looting of his own bank four years previously had come to light when he had been killed unexpectedly in an automobile accident, employed the "Translator" to explain that he had a partner in the looting of the bank—the partner being a man held in much esteem who was now a broker in Philadelphia.

Two days later, police arrested this broker. On the strength of the tip given by the banker's spook, they had located enough evidence to convict the unsuspected culprit.

At the time the broker was arrested, three strangers were present. One was an angular man with incredibly huge fists and the facial expression of a fellow who didn't have a friend in the world. The second of the trio was a lean man with the complexion of a mushroom. The third man was extremely tall and thinner than it seemed any one could be, and he had a monocle which he fingered frequently but never wore.

These three men carried credentials indicating they were special Federal agents. They did a great deal of investigating, inquiring particularly into the death of the banker years before in an automobile accident.

The three were Doc Savage's assistants, Renny, Long Tom and Johnny. That night, they talked at some length with Doc Savage via short-wave radio telephone.

"Have you," Doc Savage asked, "found anything queer?"

"Just one thing," said Renny, whose voice sounded like an angry bull in a barn. "There's a chance that the banker was murdered years ago. The automobile went off a cliff and burned. The banker was behind the wheel, but he was rumored to be unable to drive a car."

"What do you think that means?"

"Holy cow!" Renny rumbled. "I don't know, Doc. The broker helped the banker loot the bank. That's sure. Maybe the broker killed the banker so he could take all the loot."

"Have you checked on every one else connected with the case?"

"Did our best."

"Find any one who had been connected with carnivals at any time?"

"Why, yes we did, Doc. This broker's chauffeur—the chauffeur he had at the time the banker was murdered—later quit his job and went to work for carnivals."

"That," Doc Savage said, "is an interesting point."

THE arrest of the broker and the fact that enough evidence to convict him had been unearthed gave enormous added credibility to the "Static Translator."

Many newspapers had featured editorials citing incredible inventions in the past which had been hoaxes—and pointing out no less a personage than Doc Savage had said his device of Meander Surett's was worthless. After the broker-banker episode, however, such editorials disappeared. The strongest skeptics were beginning to be convinced that the machine actually worked.

Even homely Monk was doubtful.

"Doc," Monk said, "maybe we've got this wrong. You've got to admit that confounded machine hasn't done anything but good so far. Why, that poor innocent woman was released from the penitentiary, and now this guilty broker has been arrested."

"Both would appear to be desirable events," Doc Savage agreed.

Dapper Ham, who had been absent all day, returned soon after this short conversation."

"Hello, fancy britches," Monk said.

Ham ignored him.

"Doc," Ham said, "I went to this man here in Los Angeles who is accused of murdering Harold A. Beaver, and he was glad to accept my offer to serve as his lawyer."

"Hey?" Monk exploded. "What's this? You—defending the man who murdered Harold A. Beaver and let Beaver's poor widow go to the pen for the crime?"

"That's the idea," Ham said. "I managed to have his trial set for a month from to-day."

"You're a lower shyster than I thought you were!" Monk yelled. "Using your brains to get such rats out of trouble!"

"Ham is following my suggestion," Doc Savage said quietly.

"Oh!" Monk looked foolish.

"Did you ask your client the question I requested," Doc asked Ham.

Ham nodded.

"Yes," he said. "And I was surprised. Even the district attorney didn't know that Harold A. Beaver's widow used to work in carnivals."

The bronze man did a rare thing: he showed a slight amount of pleasure. His strange, trilling sound was audible for a brief moment. Then he said, "The strongest evidence against the man now accused of murdering Harold A. Beaver is the fact that he is accused of taking out the insurance policy of Beaver in the widow's name."

"Don't forget the buried murder gun!" Monk put in.

"Any one," Doc said, "can bury a gun."

Ham said, "I examined the gun. I can prove in court that it couldn't possibly have been buried over a week or two."

"Say," Monk gulped, *"what is this?"*

Doc Savage asked Ham, "What did you find on checking up on the insurance agent?"

"His bank account," Ham said, "took a mysterious five-thousand-dollar jump about two weeks ago."

"That," Doc Savage said, "is also interesting."

THE next day, the world heard about the spook of Captain Scuttle.

Captain Scuttle's spook spoke Spanish. Wrote Spanish, rather, in a jerky, huge-lettered hand. The writing was very illiterate, fully half the words being misspelled, and not a few entirely unreadable. It required half an hour for Captain Scuttle to write a short message through the medium of the "Translator." So it appeared that if a man was illiterate on earth, he died and became an illiterate spook.

Captain Scuttle was a pirate. A Spanish pirate, despite his name. That is, he had started out as a sailor in the Spanish navy, became the equivalent of an admiral, was finally assigned the job of conveying a fleet of gold-laden galleons from a Peruvian port to old Panama City, at which opportune time he turned pirate and sacked the whole fleet of gold-burdened galleons.

Captain Scuttle took half the treasure of his own, added to it some other shares he persuaded his men to let him have for safe-keeping, and hid the whole—only himself knew where. After this, he sailed away alone, intending to return later for the buried hoard. He sailed north. Off the west coast of Mexico, he was sighted by Spanish war vessels, which pursued him.

Captain Scuttle ran his war galleon ashore and fled into the jungles with his men and a small share of treasure which he had retained for capital. He was captured, staked out, and the big Mexican ants ate him. But the small treasure which he had kept for capital was never found. Neither was the big one.

Consultation of historical records verified this biography

which Captain Scuttle's spook gave of itself. It also came out that Captain Scuttle's big treasure was probably well over a hundred million dollars. This latter fact created a stir when the newspapers published it.

Not half the stir, however, that was caused when Captain Scuttle announced through the medium of Meander Surett's weird machine that he wanted to give his ill-gotten gains of three centuries ago to the benefit of Twentieth-Century humanity.

The newspapers in Paris, France, carried half a page about this, which indicated how much of an international thing the story had become.

By this time, Doc Savage was receiving no attention at all in public print. The bronze man had dropped completely out of the picture.

Which was what he was trying to do.

Daily reports came from Doc's operatives in New York—Renny, Long Tom and Johnny—indicating they could still find no trace of the real Sally Surett.

THE next day Captain Scuttle's illiterate Spanish scrawl gave the location of the small treasure in Mexico. That was at ten o'clock in the morning, and fifteen minutes after ten a fast plane was headed for the spot.

It landed at six that evening at the treasure site and was confronted by a serious-faced bunch of Mexican military men. The military men had read the telegraphic news dispatches, and gone to the spot seeking for the treasure.

They had found the treasure. The treasure was worth about ten thousand dollars. It was in doubloons and solid gold religious ornaments of ancient vintage.

The Mexican government explained politely but firmly that treasure found on Mexican soil was the national property of Mexico and would be spent to aid Mexicans.

Everett Everett Barr gave out a statement to the press in which he said he was quite delighted and the Mexican government was welcome to the treasure.

Monk read of this development back in Los Angeles and went looking for Doc Savage. Monk was carrying Habeas by one large ear, which was his habitual way of carrying his pet pig. Monk was puzzled.

"Blazes, Doc!" he complained. *"Meander Surett's machine really works!"*

Chapter XIII

MILLION-DOLLAR TREASURE

It was highly probable that no individuals with level heads had, at first, taken Meander Surett's "Static Translator" seriously, but in less than a week this initial attitude had changed completely.

The device was apparently functioning. Everything seemed honest and aboveboard. The spirits of two departed people had righted wrongs committed during their span on earth. The departed shade of a great rogue of other centuries was trying to do the same thing—and had half succeeded.

That is, Captain Scuttle had two treasures, and he had given the location of the smaller one, and it had been found. So when Captain Scuttle's spook announced it would give the location of the second treasure on the following day, the world was ripe for hundred-million-dollar news.

Ham, of course, attended the press conference during which Everett Everett Barr produced Captain Scuttle's message from Meander Surett's machine. Immediately after the conference in which Captain Scuttle's bad Spanish scrawl said the whereabouts of the big treasure would be made known to-morrow, newspapermen dashed for telephones.

Ham's dash was for Doc Savage. He told the latest news.

"I can't see what's behind this, Doc," Ham said excitedly. "Do you reckon we're all wrong about the machine?"

The bronze man began taking off his black-face make-up. It was the first time he had removed it in days.

"I think," he said, "that this affair has gone far enough.

"What do you mean, Doc?"

The bronze man was slow with his answer.

"In waiting," he said, "it begins to appear that we are playing into Everett Everett Barr's hands."

"That fellow," Ham said, "is just a cheap small-time shyster."

"You should be able to smell out a brother," Monk volunteered cheerfully.

Ham scowled.

"And speaking of smelling," Monk added, "what's become of Hoke McGee and his Lazy Y bouquets?"

"I don't know," Ham retorted. "The only one I've been seeing around is Sagebrush Smith. And that blonde girl has him hypnotized." He scowled. "She won't give me a tumble."

A moment later, Ham realized Doc Savage was studying him intently.

"You've been talking to the girl, Ham?" the bronze man asked.

Ham looked uncomfortable.

"Uh—not very much," he said hastily. "In fact—I—ah—just spoke to her."

"That's the first time I ever heard you stutter when you told a lie," volunteered the homely Monk. "Usually you do it as slick as a whistle."

"I haven't," Ham said earnestly, "done anything but merely speak to the girl."

Monk's snort, which was loud and skeptical and said plainly that the homely chemist thought the dapper lawyer was doing some dark-faced prevaricating, was merely for effect. Monk knew as well as any one that Ham was telling the truth.

"There's not a chance," Ham insisted, "that the blonde guessed who I am."

HAM was wrong. Just how wrong it became evident when, unfortunately, Ham was not in earshot. The occasion was that evening when Everett Everett Barr and the bogus Sally Surett, having evaded an increasingly attentive Sagebrush Smith, went to a remote spot for dinner.

"I've got a surprise for you, my dear husband," said the blonde.

Everett Everett Barr scowled. "I hope it's not our very good cowboy friend, Sagebrush Smith, who, if you will pardon my saying so, is showing rather more interest in you than I anticipated or approved of."

The blonde laughed.

"That clown!" she said. "He's just a big simp mesquite-jumper. You know what his ambition in life happens to be?"

"I've been wondering," said Mr. Barr jealously.

"He wants to find Doc Savage."

"I have the same ambition," said Mr. Barr grimly.

"Sagebrush Smith," the girl said, "is obsessed with the idea that he is a better shot with a six-shooter than Doc Savage. He wants to find Savage and have a shooting match to settle who is the better shot. He's a nut on that idea."

"Of course," said Mr. Barr sourly, "he isn't interested in you at all."

The blonde laughed again. "Honey," she said, "I've got a piece of news that wil take your mind off——"

She was interrupted by the appearance of Hoke McGee and his Lazy Y cowboys. Hoke and his men had entered the tiny restaurant, gotten halfway to the Barr table, and the headwaiter had stopped them and was holding his nose and gesturing for them to leave with indignation.

"It's all right," Mr. Barr interposed placatingly. "I'll rent the whole restaurant for the rest of the evening."

After this, the new arrivals seated themselves.

"Phew!" Everett Everett Barr said involuntarily.

Hoke McGee was a changed man. He had lost weight, there were hollows under his eyes, and he had a wild, hunted expression. Too, his men looked as if the hounds had been after them for some time.

"It's been a fright!" Hoke groaned.

"I can guess," said Mr. Barr.

"It wouldn't be so bad," Hoke croaked, "if we could get ourselves used to the way we smell. Blast us for coyotes! We can't even sleep with ourselves. You got no idea!"

"Where are you staying?" Everett Everett Barr asked.

"We finally hadda move out in the desert," Hoke explained gloomily. "We got holda some tents."

"It does seem that you could wash the chemical off."

"We've danged near scrubbed ourselves down to the bone." Hoke shook his head. "We went to a chemist and he says the stuff will last a week yet anyhow, and that the only stuff that would neutralize it was poisonous. We've blamed near decided to let him poison us."

Hoke McGee suddenly whipped out a six-shooter. He beat the table until glasses rolled off and broke. His eyes popped.

"If I ever see that Doc Savage again, I'll shoot his insides out!" he screamed.

"If I could find Savage for you," said Everett Everett Barr grimly, "I'd gladly let you do it."

The blonde smiled.

"What I started to say a while ago," she said, "was that I have a line on Doc Savage."

Mr. Barr lurched to his feet. "What?"

"You remember that thin-waisted Italian newspaperman?" the girl asked.

"Why, yes," said Mr. Barr. "I've noticed him examining you, my dear."

"That Italian," the girl said, "is the Doc Savage assistant known as Ham. I just figured that out to-day."

Everett Everett Barr settled back. A beatific smile overspread his countenance.

"This is wonderful," he said. "Now I have Doc Savage exactly where I want him." He chuckled. "And to think I have been doing so much worrying of late over nothing!"

THE next morning, Everett Everett Barr changed his policy. When the newspapermen assembled, he announced that Captain Scuttle's message would not be made public. What had happened to the smaller Mexican treasure made this inadvisable, he explained. If they revealed the whereabouts of the big treasure, there would obviously be an international scramble for the spot, and no telling what complications.

They would get the treasure first, explain where they got it later. But to be sure that everything was honest and aboveboard, a committee of observers would be invited to sit in and see that nothing unlawful was pulled.

The committee invited consisted of the city's leading lawyer, a representative from the Los Angeles police department, and the head of a prominent charitable institution. These persons promptly accepted.

The message from Captain Scuttle revealing whereabouts of the million-dollar treasure was brought forth in secret session.

The committee and Everett Everett Barr then announced that a week must elapse while a ship was being fitted out to go after the treasure.

Ham was present to hear the announcement. He remained in the background and carefully avoided the blonde girl's eyes, being aware that he had made an error previously in allowing his liking for attractive femininity to entice him into speaking with her a few times.

Ham's hands didn't seem to know what to do with themselves; he was accustomed to the sword cane in his hands all the time, and, of course, he was not carrying it while disguised as an Italian newspaper correspondent.

Ham left the conference with the other newshawks. As was his custom, he separated from them and headed for a near-by rooming house to report to Doc Savage.

He had walked only a few yards when he grew aware of an odor. He stopped and turned. He knew an instant later that he should have dashed into the nearest doorway and prepared for defense. But it was too late.

Hoke McGee and four of the Lazy Y men were close and showing gun snouts.

"We ain't foolin' a bit!" Hoke McGee snarled.

Ham looked at the mad light in the ranch foreman's eyes and knew he was in earnest.

"You come along with us," Hoke McGee ordered.

Ham appeared to grow terrified. He began to shake. He trembled so violently that a small bottle was dislodged from his clothing somewhere, fell on the sidewalk and broke, the liquid contents, vile yellow in color, splattering over the concrete. Ham, seemingly befuddled, stepped into the yellow mess with both feet.

"What's that yaller stuff?" Hoke McGee rasped.

"Muh-medicine for muh-my trouble," Ham croaked.

The Lazy Y foreman scowled. "What kinda trouble you got?"

"Huh—heart trouble, I guess," Ham gulped.

"That's swell!" gritted Hoke McGee. "Get movin'!"

They walked down the street to a car which was parked with the engine running, another of Hoke McGee's men behind the wheel.

"Drive to Desert Drome Airport," Hoke McGee told the chauffeur.

Ham, about to get into the car, opened his mouth wide and clutched his chest. "My heart!" he gasped. Then he collapsed, moaning, and writhed on the sidewalk. His fingers, moving in apparent agony, clawed at the concrete.

Hoke McGee picked Ham up, hurled him in the car, and the gang drove off.

DOC SAVAGE waited patiently for Ham's return. Doc had given up his eavesdropping post in Everett Everett Barr's hotel for the reason that the place had become such a focus of international newspaper interest that the scribes had started doing human interest stories about the people in the hotel. Doc was fairly certain they would learn his real identity if he lingered. He had returned to the rooming house.

Monk came in trailed by Habeas Corpus and Chemistry and said, "This is blasted funny!"

He had the newspapers containing the announcement made at the conference which Ham had attended.

"Ham should be back," Monk pointed out.

For a fractional moment, Doc Savage's strange, trilling sound seemed to pulse in the room. Then the big bronze man was at his equipment cases, extracting one of his more powerful ultra-violet ray projectors disguised as a small metal case of the type plumbers use to carry tools.

It was a dull day, threatening rain. Doc Savage and Monk donned long raincoats and large hats, brims of which they yanked down over their eyes. They set out for Everett Everett Barr's hotel.

They did not go directly to the hotel, but made a round of the block containing the hostelry. Doc kept the ultra-violet projector continuously roving the sidewalk.

They found Ham's footprints—tracks made by the yellowish stuff in which Ham had stepped deliberately. The prints, hardly noticeable to the naked eye, stood out a sulphurous color, even in the pallid daylight, when subjected to the ultra-violet rays.

"Ham—musta got—in a jam!" Monk croaked.

Considering Monk's frequently expressed intention of some day dissecting Ham, the anxiety in his tone was surprising.

Doc Savage's metallic features remained inscrutable. He followed Ham's footprints to the point where Ham had been forced to enter the car.

The writing on the sidewalk was quite readable, in view of the fact that Ham had put it there with the "invisible" chalk of Doc's invention while pretending to have a heart attack.

The message said:

Hoke McGee—me—Desert Drome Airport

DESERT DROME AIRPORT was a mushroom product of the flying craze a decade past, which had managed to survive somehow. Pilots in rickety ships gave instruction at five dollars an hour, and the hangars were full of crates that could no longer be licensed. There was a concrete take-off ramp, but it was cracked, ancient. The only pilot around the field had grease on his face.

"I ain't been payin' much attention to what went on," he said. "Got a loose rod in the engine of my bus."

Doc Savage moved over the spots where an arriving automobile would be most likely to park—and shortly he was following the sulphur-colored prints left by Ham's shoe soles, to which some of the chemical still clung.

The pilot popped his eyes at the footprints, even got down on his knees to try to discover why they disappeared when the ultra-violet light was no longer upon them.

"I don't savvy this," he muttered.

"We're followin' a ghost," Monk enlightened him.

Ham's trail led out on the ramp. And once again, Ham must have managed to get on the ground, because scrawled on the cracked concrete of the ramp they found two words:

Treasure Island

Judging from the scrawl with which the second word ended, Ham had not been given much opportunity to leave clues.

The trail ended there.

"They musta put him in a plane," Monk groaned.

Doc Savage confronted the loitering pilot. "What kind of ship took off from here within the last hour or so?"

"I dunno," the flier said, "but I think it was a two-motored low-wing job. A considerably better crate than we generally see settin' around this rookery. Oh, yes—there was a girl aboard, an invalid or somethin'."

Monk put in, "Can't you describe the plane?"

"No more'n I did," the pilot said. "There was this girl or woman who was an invalid, like I said."

Doc Savage glanced at the cloud-jammed sky, then waited patiently until the sun came out and slanted rays across the field. Crouching, moving to various positions, he studied the prints of the plane landing gear on the ramp.

He found a few grease puddles, clotted with dust, through which the wheels had passed. Farther out, where the ramp ended and the tarmac was dirt, dust stirred up by the propellers had obliterated everything.

"It was an amphibian," the bronze man said. "A large one, with a flying radius of at least two thousand miles."

Monk moved to one side. He was becoming more and more worried.

"Doc, d'you reckon them two words meant they were takin' Ham to an island where this Captain Scuttle's treasure is hidden?" the homely chemist demanded.

"That," the bronze man admitted, "is apparently the only meaning."

They went back to their rooming house.

Monk entered the door, stopped, dodged backward, crashed into Doc Savage, sat down and looked foolish.

"Holy cow!" said a voice reminiscent of a large animal in a deep cave. "You seem to have the jitters!"

"Renny!" Monk squeaked. He got to his feet foolishly. "And Long Tom and Johnny! How did you fellows get here?"

"By plane," big-voiced, big-fisted Renny explained.

"A preeminently logical eventuation," added Johnny, the long and thin geologist who never used a small word when he had time to produce a large one.

"It was this way," said Long Tom, the deceptively unhealthy-looking electrical wizard. "We've been working our heads off in New York, and finally got trace of the real Sally Surett. She is being held prisoner, and has been for several weeks."

"Then what're you doin' here?" Monk demanded.

"The girl," Long Tom said, "was put on a plane in New York yesterday and rushed here to Los Angeles. We trailed the ship and just got in. We've been telephoning airports trying to locate it here in Los Angeles."

Doc Savage asked, "Was it a large two-motored amphibian?"

"Why," said Long Tom, "how did you know that?"

"The same plane," Doc Savage said, "took off within the last hour or so with two prisoners aboard. The captives were Ham and a girl who was mistaken for an invalid by the men at the airport."

"That invalid," Monk surmised, "was the real Sally Surett. They got her doped or something." The homely chemist stared at the bronze man. "Doc, we gotta do somethin' drastic. This thing, whatever it is, is comin' to a head and we're just jumpin' around grabbin' at thin air."

"Bring in your portable chemical laboratory," Doc Savage said quietly, "and we will start operations."

THE committee of a lawyer, a police official and the head of a charitable institution, which was to observe the honesty of the search for Captain Scuttle's treasure, got together for a dinner that evening at the lawyer's home. They wanted to get better acquainted with each other, since they were to be associated closely.

Dinner was served in the large walnut-paneled dining room. In the middle of the meal, something unexpected happened.

Every one went to sleep.

The police official slumped forward, buried his face in his soup and made bubbling noises.

Doc Savage threw wide the window through which he and Monk, the chemist, had put anæsthetic gas into the room. The bronze man climbed in, lifted the policeman out of his soup so he wouldn't drown, then got a hypodermic needle out of a metal case and began administering chemical peparations to the three victims.

Monk, Renny, Long Tom and Johnny climbed into the room while he was doing this.

"D'you reckon it was necessary," Monk muttered, "to

gas 'em, then use truth serum to get the information we want? Maybe they'd 'a' told us if we just asked 'em."

"These men," Doc Savage said, "are noted publicity-seekers. Their sympathies, moreover, are with Everett Everett Barr. It is hardly likely they would have given us much consideration, particularly in view of the way the newspapers have been knocking us lately."

The bronze man completed his administrations. The anæsthetic gas, colorless and odorless, was virtually an adjunct to the truth serum, coördinating its effects with that of the serum, which rendered the subjects semiconscious and obliterated conscious control of their faculties—in short, made them unable to remember to tell a lie, or to remember to refuse to answer questions.

Doc's first question: "Do you think Everett Everett Barr is honest and the Meander Surett machine actually genuine?"

"Yes," was the answer from all three.

"Which means they're not dupes of Barr," Monk muttered.

Doc's second question: "Where is the treasure of Captain Scuttle located?"

"On Scorn Island, off the coast of Lower California," was the answer to this. "It is sunken in the small cove on the east shore, and not in the large cove on the west shore."

"Where's a map?" Monk muttered. "I never heard of any Scorn Island."

"Scorn Island," Doc Savage said, "is three miles long, half a mile wide, has a maximum altitude of seven hundred feet, and is largely barren, the principal vegetation being cactus and mesquite. The island is located about thirty miles off the eastern, or barren side of the peninsula of Lower California."

THE bronze man's four associates showed no surprise that he should have an encyclopedic fund of information concerning an island of which none of them had ever heard. They were quite well acquainted with the fact that his mind held an incredible array of knowledge.

"How are we gonna keep these three fellows from suspecting something queer happened to them?" Renny rumbled.

Doc Savage managed that quite simply. He removed all traces of the visit of himself and his men, this consisting principally in sponging away the drop or two of red leakage from the pricks of the hypodermic needle. Then he opened the jets of the gas heater and let enough gas into the house to make a perceptible odor, but not enough to endanger any one's life. Then he called the fire department.

From across the street, the bronze man watched the fire department arrive and rush the three victims off to receive treatment for imaginary gassing. A little later in the night, they would awaken, none the worse for an experience, no detail of which they would be able to remember.

"Did you bring the big plane from New York?" Doc asked.

"Yes," Renny admitted.

"Get it ready for a flight to Scorn Island," Doc directed, "while Monk and myself pick up our equipment." Then after a moment the bronze man added, "We will leave Habeas and Chemistry behind in care of our landlady. I don't think it would be advisable to bring them along where we're going."

Chapter XIV

SCORN ISLAND

THE plane was bronze-colored. It had a wing span of the big sleeper ships used on the transcontinental air lines, but lacked the bulk of the flying arks on the transatlantic or transpacific runs. It could alight and take off from land or water, and was a really remarkable ship with probably its most unusual feature being the streamlining.

The craft was internationally famous; almost any one posted on aëronautics would recognize it as Doc Savage's latest design, the bronze man's private speed job, built to his own specifications.

The night was dark over the seven-hundred-fifty-mile long claw of land snapped down from the California-Mexico border that was Lower California. On the western coast it was cool, typically pleasant California climate; but on the eastern coast, over which the plane flew, there was furnace heat even at an altitude of three thousand feet.

There were clouds at ten thousand, but their wadded whiteness did not promise rain. They merely shut out the moonlight occasionally.

Both motors of the big bronze plane were silenced so effectively that at three thousand feet its passing was hardly audible to night-riding *vaqueros* or such *caballeros* as were abroad this late. Occasionally night-flying *golondrinas* darted aside in fright as the great man-bird of alloy metals arrowed across a rift in the clouds.

The plane banked a little, changing course, leaving even these few signs of civilization. Soon the rutty *caminos* no longer snaked below, and there were no fine *casas,* and not even a miserable sheep-tender's hut. Only desert inhabited by the stinging *alacran* and the fierce-biting red ant called *hormiga.*

Then came a coast line as unlovely as a scab, and beyond that the Gulf of Lower California—fishing waters for tuna, shark and the barracudas that eat men.

A hump appeared on the sea, a hump longer than wide. Scorn Island. It was volcanic rock, a little less brittle than glass, about as fertile. A cove took a bite out of one side of Scorn Island; a bay gouged the other side.

Bow windows of the plane looked down like eyes. The ship settled over the larger cove, and light jumped in great white whiskers from the landing floods, and the motors idled and coughed sparks. The ship lined down at the waves.

With coughs and snorts, sheets of spray shot from under the hull. The ship bucked, rocked and bumped its belly on wave tops at sixty miles an hour. The impacts came back from the rock-walled sides of the bay like deep drumbeats.

Having landed, the plane sat idle for a few moments; then the rudder wagged, the propellers blew back a cloud of spray and the craft headed in slowly toward the beach.

The plane was about fifty yards off-shore when the speed boat appeared. The speed boat headed straight for the big plane, gathering velocity. A man stood up in the stern of the speed boat and jumped overboard.

The boat, still gaining speed, hit the plane going fully thirty miles an hour.

Gore-red flame jumped two hundred feet in the night. Concussion flatted the bay water. Shock rolled boulders on the sides of the lava island. A gigantic geyser of blasted water climbed up and up until it seemed it would never stop, and mixed in with this brine and foam and smoke were the dissected remains of Doc Savage's great plane.

THE fabulous blast had stunned the man who had aimed the speed boat, then jumped overboard. He made croaking noises, waved his arms, and as flashlight beams ran out to him from shore his arms gesticulated like the legs of a hurt fly on its back.

Hoke McGee jumped around on shore and shouted, "Somebody save 'im! I can't swim!"

Men plunged in and swam out to the injured man and dragged him ashore. When they hauled the fellow out on the stony beach, he cursed Hoke McGee with feeble vituperation.

"I thoughtcha said five cases of dynamite wouldn't stun me!" was his refrain.

Hoke McGee ignored the man. Stalking to the edge of the water, the Lazy Y foreman shook his fist at the patch of bubbles, spreading oil and floating life-preserver cushions which was all the evidence that remained of the great bronze plane.

"That fixes up Doc Savage!" he squawled.

He continued to shake his fist, and he swore for four minutes without repeating anything but the name of Doc Savage.

"Puttin' that stinkin' stuff on us was funny, eh?" he yelled violently at the spot where the plane had come apart in flame. "I bet you don't think it was clever now!"

One of the Lazy Y cowhands came over to him.

"You gone batty, standin' there whoopin' at the water? The smell's gone, so what's the use of talkin' about it?" the cowhand wanted to know.

"Shut up!" Hoke said. "This is one of my high points. Danged if I've had many lately!"

The Lazy Y foreman contemplated the smear of oil with grisly delight. When the life-preserved cushions floated ashore, he ran to one, seized it and turned his flashlight on the small monogram "DOC" which it bore.

"A souvenir!" he whooped. "He had the world buffaloed, but it took old Hoke McGee to feed him to the fishes!"

Hoke was delighted. He did everything but beat his chest and roar. After which he whirled, stamped into a cleft among the lava boulders, passing the amphibian which had brought him and his men to the island and which had been drawn up out of the water into concealment.

A hundred yards beyond the plane, Hoke McGee blazed

the beam of his flashlight into the eyes of Ham Brooks. Ham was bound.

"You hear the firecracker a few minutes ago?" Hoke demanded.

Ham swallowed. He was pale.

"That," Hoke said, "was the finish of that guy they called the man of bronze."

Ham said nothing. But he grew rigid.

Hoke McGee strode onward a few yards and stood frowning at a second bound figure—that of a small, dark-haired girl with attractive features.

"Barr was a dope for keepin' you around so long," Hoke told the girl. "He thought he might need you to sign some papers or somethin' to help put over the hoax of Barr's wife bein' you. Hell, that was more precaution than he needed to take!"

"I've been trying to decide," the girl said coldly, "whether you're a worse rat than the others, or whether you're all about alike."

Hoke McGee drew back a foot.

A Lazy Y cowhand interrupted, "I kinda hate to see women kicked around, Hoke."

"You wouldn't be givin' me orders?" Hoke snarled.

"No," said the other. "I'm just tellin' you I'll shoot your teeth out if you beat up this girl Sally Surett."

Hoke stuck out his jaw. But he also withdrew his foot. True to his policy of never doing any unnecessary fighting face-to-face, he made a mental note to have the dissenter in front of him, where a bullet might hit the fellow—accidentally of course—in case there was another fight.

Hoke went back to Ham.

"Everythin' is mighty nice now," he said. "Nothin' can slip. Old Double-Everetts is aboard a little steamer he's chartered for the treasure hunt, and he and his party will be down here in three or four days."

Ham frowned. "The treasure is really on this island?"

'Sure." Hoke McGee then laughed queerly.

"What kind of infernal thing are you birds planning?" Ham demanded.

"Partner," Hoke said, "it's a honey. And the most honeyed thing about it is that you and that girl and a dead man are gonna be blamed for what finally happens."

"Dead man?" Ham muttered.

"I mean Doc Savage," Hoke said. "He's probably pretty dead by now."

FOR a dead man, Doc Savage was exerting a good deal of strength. His cabled arms tightened, strained, and with such metallic hardness did the sinews stand out that the bronze skin seemed to vanish and show incredible ligature development.

The gyroplane creaked quietly, lifted, came free of the lava crevice which had trapped one wheel when the ship sank quietly out of the sky and made a landing that had been too rough because of the necessity of making it without the aid of the engine. Silence had been important.

Monk looked at Renny, and Renny looked at Monk. Physically, they were the most powerful of Doc Savage's group of associates. Both of them had been straining at the wheel to make the lift the bronze man had just made—and hadn't budged it at all.

"There really wasn't room for two men to lift at once," Doc remarked.

Monk and Ham knew differently. Doc had managed alone what their combined strength could not accomplish.

"I'm afraid they maybe heard us land," muttered Long Tom, who looked almost like a hospital case and yet could lick nine out of any ten men he would meet on the street.

"A dubitative point of polemicality," said Johnny seriously.

"Will somebody," Monk requested, "translate that?"

"He thinks it's doubtful they heard us," Long Tom explained.

Doc's associates shouldered the plane around, moved it over against a mass of lava bowlders and backed it in between two of the rocks that offered a natural hangar for the plane.

Long Tom, the electrical wizard, remembered something and grunted.

"I forgot to switch off the radio-control transmitter we were using to guide the big plane," he explained.

He climbed into the plane and cut off the battery power from the complicated radio device, similar to the experimental machines with which military men guide pilotless airplane bombs.

"I don't figure they know we're here," Long Tom

said, climbing out again. "They wouldn't expect another plane, and we stayed up against the clouds when we brought the big plane down on the bay by radio." He scowled. "They sure blew up a good ship for us. Doc, how'd you know they were planning that?"

"Not being a clairvoyant," said the bronze man, "I could hardly know what they planned. But Everett Everett Barr has been very clever and careful so far. It was reasonable to believe they would have plans for a reception, should we trace Ham to the island. That's why I secretly had this gyroplane hidden in case I should need it."

Doc's aids busied themselves getting equipment out of the plane: gas grenades, the terrific little machine-pistols which fired the highly explosive slugs or "mercy bullets" producing quick, harmless unconsciousness. There was also gas masks, chain-mesh outer cloaks of an alloy metal which would turn anything short of a bullet from a tank-rifle, and photo-electric mechanical devices for seeing in intense darkness with the aid of invisible wave lengths of light.

"Hey!" hairy Monk grunted. "Doc's gone!"

THE bronze man, the aids discovered, had faded away with the silence which was characteristic.

"Psst!" Monk hissed. "Doc!"

There was no answer.

"Psst!" Monk said, more loudly. "Doc, where——"

"You trying to raise the whole island?" Long Tom whispered. "Doc is probably scouting around."

Monk snorted. "There ain't no need of any scouting. We know them mugs are down on the shore of the big bay. All we gotta do is go get Ham."

They talked the matter over.

"I'm in favor," Monk insisted, "of getting right over to that bay."

The idea of action appealed to Renny, Long Tom and Johnny. They had been in New York during most of Doc Savage's difficulties so far with Meander Surett's chest, and they had done dull detective work until they were amply filled up on such stuff. They loved excitement.

In fact, two things really held them in close association with the bronze man, and money was *not* one of the things, each being comparatively wealthy in his own right, or capable of making enormous fees in his chosen profession. They liked excitement, action, danger—and that was one of the two binding threads. The other was their admiration for the man of bronze and the strange work he was doing.

Having decided to go ahead with rescuing Ham, the aids left a note to that effect on the plane for Doc Savage when he returned. Then they set out across the island.

They wore rubber-soled footgear, and the terrain was almost exclusively hard lava rock, so they had little trouble with noise. Monk went ahead. Second to Doc Savage, he could move with the greatest stealth.

Ham had always insisted this was because Monk's ancestors had obviously come down out of the trees several hundred centuries after the rest of humanity.

Coming close to the bay, Monk went ahead and investigated. He was back shortly.

"They got a camp under a cliff," he breathed. "Ham is tied up there, and some girl—probably the real Sally Surett."

After conferring, the bronze man's helpers concluded to advance and look over the situation. Meantime, Doc Savage should show up.

"Take it easy!" Monk breathed.

They crept forward.

HOKE MCGEE stood over Ham. The Lazy Y foreman had removed the barrel from a rifle, and he was engaged in two pursuits: He was carefully nursing up a hot fire out of desert island shrubs, and he was tapping Ham over the head with the rifle barrel. He was hitting Ham just about as hard as he could without causing unconsciousness.

"You're wasting your time!" Ham croaked painfully.

Hoke McGee gave him another blow with the rifle barrel.

"I've found out," Hoke snarled, "that Doc Savage has all the gold he wants. He gets it from somewhere, and he's been gettin' it for years. I wanta know where it comes from!"

"Nothing doing," Ham said.

Hoke McGee scowled, slugged with the rifle barrel. Ham made a strangled noise and collapsed.

"He's throwed a Joe," a cowhand muttered. "You hit 'im too hard."

Hoke McGee began heating the rifle barrel in the fire.

"This'll bring 'im out of it!" he growled.

Monk crouched against the black flank of a near-by boulder, and his arms began to tremble, so tight were his muscles. In spite of their perpetual squabbling, he and Ham were the closest friends. Monk, watching what was happening, was infinitely more enraged than if he had been in Ham's place.

Hoke McGee wadded his battered five-gallon hat and used it to hold the end of the heating rifle barrel. When he eventually drew it from the flame, the steel was red with heat. He approached Ham.

"I'll go to work on one of his eyes," he muttered. "That'll wake 'im up!"

Rage that was stronger than any sense of caution sent Monk hurtling out into the firelight. Bullet head back, mouth agape, great furry half-dollar-crushing hands distended, the chemist charged. He made roaring noises as he came. His fights were always noisy.

Like the fox he resembled, Hoke McGee could move by instinct. Before the reasoning part of his brain could possibly telegraph a message, he could evade a danger. It was instinct that made him hurl the hot rifle barrel blindly at Monk. Instinct sent him pitching for—not the outer darkness—but for the small tent which comprised the camp. He pitched into the tent.

The interval during which Hoke McGee was inside the tent was hardly more than ten seconds. During the time, there was a loud crash of glass. Then Hoke McGee opened the back of the tent from ground cloth to eave with a bowie knife and went out through the back.

"Run, men!" he bellowed. "Run!"

He set an example. The darkness took him. Others followed. Two of his men got up out of blankets near the fire and the darkness took them, too.

MONK was full of red rage. He craved fight. And there was suddenly no one around to fight. The homely chemist bellowed. He bounded up and down. He kicked the fire to the winds and upset a bucket of water on the embers so that the light would not target him.

"C'mon and fight!" he squawked.

"You hairy clown," Ham said feebly. "Come on and untie me."

Monk fell upon the knots which bound the lawyer and said, "I don't see why I didn't let 'em go ahead and fix you up, you shyster!"

"Where did Hoke go?" Ham demanded.

"In one end of the tent and out the other, kickin' over glassware as he went," Monk explained.

"Glassware?"

"I heard somethin' break."

"Oh, murder!" Ham croaked. "Run, Monk! Run! Leave me!"

"Leave nothin'," Monk said. "In a minute——"

"Run!" Ham screamed. *"Run!"*

"But——"

"You don't get it, Monk!" Ham shrieked. "They had a five-gallon container of gas! Intended using it if the dynamite didn't get Doc——"

He began to cough. Monk, suddenly understanding that Hoke McGee must have broken the gas container in the tent, seized Ham, carried him. He started coughing. He stumbled a dozen paces with Ham, and their coughing got worse; and then they fell down and beat their chests, held their throats, and their coughing became terrible.

The other aids ran up and tried to help them, but they were coughing, too, and seemed weak, for they were unable to either help or run away. They went down, and squirmed, and their writhing grew weaker; and then they stopped moving altogether.

Doc Savage, coming down the canyon, drawn by their cries, saw their huddled forms. It was quite dark. He was using a projector of light rays outside the visible spectrum, and a complicated viewer device for his eyes—a contrivance of mirrors which received a semi-fluorescent picture formed by impact of the reflected "black light" on a chemical coating which retained the image long enough for it to be turned and shown to the bronze man's eyes.

The apparatus was in theory like a camera which took a picture with infra-rays, then showed the picture to the bronze man's eyes—a picture which faded instantly, and another took its place.

The slumped forms of his men told him what had

happened. Gas! Doc removed the "black light" viewer. He pulled a gasproof hood over his head which contained a "mechanical lung" for breathing purposes. Then he went on. It was very dark now, except when he held the viewer to his eyes—the harness of the device would not fit over the mask.

Suddenly he stumbled. He got up—stumbled again. He stopped. The gas! It was some kind that was effective through the skin pores!

Realizing that, Doc turned and tried to retrace his steps. Once more he went down. This time, he could not get up. He tried to crawl.

The best he could do was drag himself into a lava crack and get off the mask. Then existence became grisly blackness.

Chapter XV

TREASURE SHIP

THE sun was hot. Hot as it could get on these barren islands where coolness and moisture of the Pacific Ocean was cut off by the great bald finger of Lower California. It must have been well over a hundred and thirty in the lava crack where the bronze man lay. Enough perspiration was in his eyes to sting. Wetness of it was all over him.

Doc Savage did not stir for some time after consciousness returned. During the interval, his mind, clinical by habit, analyzed effects and symptoms and decided on the kind of gas which had overcome him. He had used that type himself on occasions.

His men would not have died from the gas.

What had happened to them after they had been gassed was problematical. How long had Doc himself been here? His knowledge of the gas indicated the effects lasted as much as three days.

The bronze man tried to get up, and stiffness, weakness, and aches told him the maximum of three days must have elapsed.

Obviously, Hoke McGee's men had not found him. He still wore the unusual carry-all vest containing his equipment. He searched in it for a strength stimulant in tablet form, and ate two of the tablets slowly.

In fifteen minutes, Doc could move with some freedom, although his mouth was dry and his lips withered. In spite of the deep bronze coloring which tropical suns had given his skin, he had been sunburned. He went looking for his men—went cautiously, keeping always under cover, which was not easy.

They were gone. Hoke McGee, his cowhands, the tent, their plane, Monk, Ham, Renny, Long Tom, Johnny, Sally Surett—everything and everybody was gone. They might have been moved to some other part of the cove.

But after the bronze man had made a complete round of the bay, he was sure they had left that part of the island.

He went back to the spot where Hoke McGee's crew had camped, and found dried bloodstains where his men—dead or alive—must have been thrown together. He used a diminutive ultra-violet ray projector which he took from his vest, but its projection was not as strong as the large one and the brilliant sun defeated it until he removed his shirt and made a tiny tent, after which he found the message in big-worded Johnny's handwriting. But this time Johnny had used small words:

DOC: WE MADE THEM BELIEVE YOU DIED
IN PLANE BLAST

That was all. Nothing to show what had happened to the prisoners. Nothing to indicate whether they were still alive or whether they had been thrown into the bay for the sharks.

The bronze man went back to the bay and watched the water, knowing that sharks were inclined to remain around a spot where they had been well fed. There were a great number of sharks, like flexible slime-gray logs.

Metallic features lined and grim, the bronze man turned and went back inland to his gyroplane. To what remained, rather—the fire-blackened metal corpse would never fly again. The craft had been found, systematically demolished, and the parts—such of them as could be used again—smashed. All equipment had been demolished, broken or burned.

There was only one large general equipment box left which Doc had removed from the plane and concealed prior to leaving it—a precaution which he habitually took and which had served him in good stead before.

Of the most needed thing, there was none. No water. He had to have water. He began collecting sheets of plane metal and copper fuel-line with the idea of making a water still and firing it with island shrubs to distill fresh water from the sea brine. He was working on it when the whistle of a steamer whooped three times in excited haste.

Doc Savage headed toward the sound.

THE steamer had been built back in the days when people thought a three-hundred-footer was quite a craft. Any one not knowing about salt-water ravage would have thought she had not been painted since, whereas, she had really been painted the last time but two or three years past. Smoke crawled straight up from one funnel which was slightly askew; and cargo booms, masts and cables, looked like a nest started by a crazy bird.

The old hooker lay in the little cove. The water was evidently very deep, because she was held, not by anchors, but by rusting wire cables sprung out to either shore. The cove was small.

Two lifeboats were afloat in the cove. Everett Everett Barr stood in one; Sagebrush Smith and the blonde girl were in the other. Men manned the oars of each dory.

A dozen men dressed in whites and helmets lounged under deck canopies on the steamer. A man in dirty overalls and an officer's cap was whooping through a megaphone.

"The radio operator," he bawled, "has picked up the short-wave signals of an airplane, and he says, judgin' from the strength of the signals, it's blasted close!"

"Who's in the plane?" Everett Everett Barr shouted.

"Somebody named Hoke McGee!" roared the steamer officer. "He's askin' if the steamer has reached the island yet. We didn't answer, figurin' he was maybe somebody who is tryin' to grab old Cap'n Scuttle's treasure."

"Tell him we're here, you fool!" Everett Everett Barr bellowed.

"But——"

"Hoke McGee"—Mr. Barr was squawling angrily—"is a man I hired to come ahead by plane and watch this island to see nobody got the treasure before we arrived!"

"I didn't know——"

"D'you think I tell everybody my plans?" Barr roared.

"You tell Hoke McGee we're here. He knows where the island is. He came here four days ago. I guess he's been stayin' at another island so as not to call anybody's attention to this one."

The man with the megaphone went away from the rail.

Doc Savage hurried back to the equipment case which he had hidden near his burned gyroplane. From it he got fresh oxygen cartridges for his gas mask, which would serve also as a diving "lung."

He returned to the small cove, inserted the oxygen cartridge and donned the mask. The sides of the cove were rocky enough to make it easy to enter the water unobserved.

JUST before Doc submerged, he turned over his wrist watch to expose the luminous-dialed compass which was on the back of the watch. He took bearing on the steamer.

He turned on his back, swam out and down, touching the bottom frequently, until pressure told him that he was as deep as it was safe to go without a pressure-proof suit.

Doc had hoped to swim all the way to a point below the steamer and keep on the bottom where there was less danger from sharks—less because they could only attack from above and the sides. He swam carefully, turning, watching—and suddenly saw a shark.

Length of the shark must have been sixteen feet, and even that was not large for these waters. The bronze man came to a standstill, paddling only enough to keep natural buoyancy from lifting him to the surface. From a pocket of his carry-all vest he took a bottle which he had brought from the equipment case. He opened this and shook out the contents, a liquid.

Meanwhile, the shark came closer, circled once, then flicked its tail and came down for the bronze man. The water was clear, and the shark's open mouth seemed to hold a million teeth.

Ten feet from the bronze man, the shark put on the brakes. Then it turned wildly and fled.

Doc swam on, leaving the protection of the chemical which he had put into the water—a chemical the result of a careful study of what sharks, barracudas and other sea-killers were most afraid of.

It was the *physalia* type of giant sea organism, a thing

like a plucked-up mass of purplish roots which had stinging, paralyzing properties, smaller cousins to the things called Portuguese Man of War along the Gulf coast of the United States. The chemical merely gave the water the subtle bite of the presence of the *physalia.* It terrified the sharks as the smell of a lion terrifies horses.

Doc could have fought the shark with a knife—and been betrayed by the rising blood to those on board the steamer.

A few minutes later, Doc Savage was feeling along the barnacle-warted bottom of the old steamer. He came up close to the rudder.

A glance showed that the plane had appeared and was circling, intending to land outside the cove and taxi to the steamer. The two lifeboats had returned to the steamer, and the occupants had already climbed ladders to the deck. It was fairly certain every one would be on the seaward side of the ship, watching the arrival of the plane.

Doc Savage uncoiled his collapsible grapple and silk cord from inside his shirt. He snared the rail with his first toss of the rubber-silenced grapple. He climbed.

Reaching the rail, he lifted for a cautious survey. No one in sight. Swinging over the side, he made for a companionway and dropped down it. Heat of the sun almost instantly dried what faint wet footprints he made.

THE old steamer had smells below. Strong smells. Odors remindful of bananas, hides, guano, copra and plain dirt. Oil reek from her engines fumigated her from stem to stern. Below, she was not a place where men stayed when they did not have to.

Doc Savage encountered no one as he worked to the seaward side and found a porthole. With the ball of a thumb, he cleaned a patch large enough for a peephole.

The plane had landed, and was being drifted tail-first toward one of the cargo booms which had been run out to serve as a picket post for the craft. Men were hurling lines, missing, and hurling again. Hoke McGee was standing on the teetering plane wing, doing his customary skillful swearing.

The plane was eventually made fast to the end of the boom.

Doc Savage listened to men who were standing on the deck directly above him.

"This'll make a good color story for the final editions," said one of the voices. "Get pictures of 'em as they come off the plane, Sam."

Newspapermen, from their conversation.

"Who's this Hoke McGee?"

"All I know is that Barr said he's a man they hired."

"Seems to be a crowd in the plane."

"Yeah. They're comin' aboard now—— Hey! Great blazes! You see what I see?"

"Their hands are tied. Five men and a girl, all with their hands tied!"

"Sam!" exploded one journalist. "Snap that! Snap a picture quick! *Those prisoners are Doc Savage's men!*"

Excitement seized the newspapermen. They swarmed to the rail, yelling questions. It was some moments before Hoke McGee quieted them with profanity.

"Of course they're Doc Savage's gang!" Hoke bellowed. "They came down here by plane three days ago!"

"But——"

"Tried to grab the treasure! We captured 'em!"

Punctuating with picturesque vituperative, Hoke described an imaginary and inhuman raid by Doc Savage's men upon his camp on the island. Then he went into detailed length about a fight in which Doc Savage's men had been gassed and captured.

"We're gonna take 'em back to Los Angeles, and demand they stand trial for attempted murder and piracy!" Hoke bellowed.

"Where is Doc Savage?" a newspaperman demanded.

Hoke had an answer ready for that.

"We ran Savage off," Hoke declared. "But he swore he'd come back and get that gold if he hadda get rid of everybody around here."

"That doesn't sound like Doc Savage," a journalist remarked.

"I'm just tellin' you what happened," Hoke said virtuously. "Ask any of my men if I ain't right."

There was an avalanche of questions from the newspapermen, but Everett Everett Barr, interrupting with polite firmness, insisted that the prisoners be committed to the ship's brig, after which he and Hoke McGee would confer. Later, the journalists could interview to their hearts' content.

This was done.

DOC SAVAGE watched the incarcerating of the captives from the end of a corridor. He noted that two guards were placed in front of the barred cabins with rifles. It was very hot, and the guards were naked to the waist.

Monk, the homely chemist, was in a great rage. He did some bellowing at the top of his voice.

"This is all a dirty plot of some kind!" Monk squawled. "That machine of Meander Surett's won't work. Old Meander Surett was touched in the head. This Barr is pullin' a shenanigan!"

Renny, Long Tom, Johnny and Ham were quieter. The small pretty girl, Sally Surett, had nothing to say.

Monk roared, "Lemme tell you newspaper guys exactly what happened! This girl is——"

The homely chemist went silent—for Doc Savage had tensed his throat and said one word, and it had seemed to come from the group of newspapermen, thanks to Doc's command of ventriloquial effects.

The word was not one that Sally Surett, Everett Everett Barr or any of the newspapermen understood. It was ancient Mayan for "Quiet!" and Doc Savage and his aids were among the few people in the so-called civilized world who could speak the tongue.

The prisoners had nothing more to say, and the one-word command attracted no attention. Everett Everett Barr thought some one had cleared a throat.

"Gentlemen," said Mr. Barr to the newspapermen, "I am now going to confer with my old pal, my old friend here, the Honorable Hoke McGee. Come on, Hoke, my associate, my comrade, my good man."

Hoke McGee strutted at Everett Everett Barr's side, and they went to the latter's cabin. But they were trailed by persistent journalists, and there was some confusion and a delay and finally the impatient newshawks had to be locked out of Mr. Barr's cabin.

"There's another door," Barr told Hoke. "I'll lock it, too."

The cabin was part of a suite of rooms, all with doors opening into the corridor. Barr closed the connecting door to the adjacent cabin, then sat down on a bunk and wiped his face with a handkerchief.

"Thank the dickens that's over," he muttered. "Getting those prisoners aboard was a critical point."

"I was afraid they'd do a lot of talkin'," Hoke muttered. "And them hombres can bulldog words, believe me. That dang lawyer can talk the knob off a door. They might've sold the newspaper mugs the truth."

"Don't worry," Mr. Barr said. "Everything is now set."

THE cabin was stuffy, and Barr turned on a fan. Breeze from the fan rippled the overhanging edges of the oilcloth cover on the one table in the place, stirred the grimy curtain over the porthole. There was one locker, a dresser, three chairs, and a blowsy rug on the floor. Hoke McGee licked his lips.

"You sure," he muttered, "that it'll go through? It's kinda complicated."

"Hoke, old pal, old sock, the machines which do the finest work are the complicated ones, and as long as the parts are well designed and put together, it makes no difference how complicated the machine is."

"Um-m-m."

"I worked on this for months," Barr said. "I began working on it when little Miss Sally Surett showed me letters from her father, letters which said he had perfected his 'Static Translator.' "

"When did you first know the 'Static Translator' was of no account?" Hoke demanded.

"Why, from the very first. Sally Surett knew her father was mentally unbalanced, and guessed that he only imagined he had perfected his device. Later, of course, Bill Horder found the Death Valley laboratory and made sure the contrivance wouldn't work."

"You're pretty slick," Hoke admitted.

Somewhere in the old steamer, a motor generator set started pounding and whining. Heat steamed into the cabins of the vessel. Both Hoke and Barr wielded handkerchiefs.

"Hoke, old top," said Mr. Barr, "it was a good scheme. It still is. Meander Surett was to be found dead in the desert, and his invention discovered. Then I was to take the invention and by a clever series of fake demonstrations, make it seem genuinely workable. That, substantially, is what has happened—in spite of the intervention of Doc Savage."

"Damn that guy!" Hoke gritted. "Thank blazes he's croaked!"

"You're *sure* about the croaking?"

"Plumb positive."

Barr sighed relief. "Everything played into my hands, Hoke, my colleague. Take the case of Harold Beaver's widow, who was in the penitentiary. She really killed her husband. She sent word to me, an old carnival acquaintance, that she would pay me five thousand dollars to get her out. There, Hoke, my boy, was a ready-made job for Meander Surett's machine.

"I merely buried the murder gun—the whereabouts of which Harold Beaver's widow told me—under the late Harold Beaver's business partner's garage. Then I paid the insurance agent to say the partner had taken the policy out on Beaver's life to throw suspicion on the widow. Presto! I had a situation all ready for a ghost message."

Barr presented a cigarette case combined with lighter, barometer and thermometer. "Have a smoke?"

"Thanks."

Barr inhaled smoke luxuriously. "The other case, the one of the broker and banker, was a genuine dyed-in-the-wool murder all ready for revealing." He chuckled. "I knew of it because the broker's chauffeur, who knew his boss murdered the banker and helped loot the bank, afterward worked for me in a carnival. He got drunk once and the story—er—leaked out."

"Yeah," Hoke said, "but there ain't no Captain Scuttle, the pirate."

"Only we know that, Hoke, old soak."

"But there ain't no treasure, neither."

EVERETT EVERETT BARR fell to chuckling. "There was one treasure: The small one. They say it is worth ten thousand dollars. That's a lie. It cost me nearly fifteen thousand to buy those old coins and old gold crosses, vases and stuff which composed it. It cost me another five hundred to fly down and bury it."

"You spent a lot of dough," Hoke mumbled.

"Twenty thousand or so. Not much, when the stake is two hundred and ninety-eight thousand dollars."

"That what you got?"

"Yes." Barr sighed regretfully. "If I had dared wait another day or two, I could have made it half a million, I really do believe."

The two men ground out their cigarettes and mopped their faces.

"I'm sure surprised," Hoke said, "that people would put up that much dough to finance the search for Captain Scuttle's treasure."

"Hoke, old bird," said Barr, "I knew human nature from my carnival experience. People will gamble their money on the chance of getting a big stake. I made the stake in this plenty big. One hundred million, you remember my carefully prepared 'Static Translator' messages said."

"How much did you have to pay out to charter this boat?"

"Only three thousand for the ship and a number of large boxes which are supposed to contain expensive diving equipment," Barr explained. "The two hundred and ninety-eight thousand is net profit, Hoke, my brother."

"Not bad," Hoke said, and licked his lips, "if the rest goes all right."

"It will go all right," Barr declared. "In about five minutes, we will finish it."

"That quick?"

"Of course. Hold off court troubles. Doc Savage's men might get out, you know."

"Then I take it we're all fixed?"

EVERETT EVERETT BARR nodded gravely. "There are one hundred cases of dynamite in the hold, all fused and ready to blow up." Barr chuckled. "The dynamite is in the boxes supposed to contain diving equipment."

"But suppose it blows us up——"

"Not a chance," Barr interrupted. "The sailors are going to start a fight. They will shout that Doc Savage's men have escaped. You and I and my wife will dash to the plane and cast off. The men will take to the boats, after lighting the fuse.

"The dynamite will tear the ship to pieces, and Doc

Savage's men will be drowned—because they will be locked in the brig. We will simply say that they must have blown the ship up accidentally."

"But," Hoke pointed out, "the birds who financed the search with that two hundred and ninety-eight thousand dollars will want us to make another try for Captain Scuttle's treasure."

"Let them," Barr said. "We won't worry."

"But——"

"We are going to disappear. Vanish, and enjoy our profits."

"But your law business——"

"Unfortunately," said Mr. Barr, "I was about to be disbarred."

"Suppose the 'Static Translator' is found?"

"What if it is found? It will go down with the ship, of course. It is very unlikely to be found. This cove is extremely deep. I made sure of that weeks ago in a search for a suitable island."

Hoke scratched his head, mopped his face and made faces of a man thinking everything over.

"Yeah, I guess," he muttered finally. "But say, you never did tell me exactly how you got the fake messages out of old Surett's contraption."

"They came," said Mr. Barr, "out of the additional piece of apparatus. I never did exhibit the contents of that device. It was merely a clockwork which pushed out messages previously prepared." Barr got to his feet. "We are talking over trivialities now. Hoke, old ranny, old waddy, old cow-wrangler, the future beckons. Let us be up and at it."

"You mean—sink the ship now?"

"Exactly."

Hoke made an audible swallowing noise. He followed Everett Everett Barr out of the cabin.

Doc Savage opened the door of the locker from which he had been listening to all that had been said. The bronze man left the cabin by the side door—the same route by which he had entered under cover of the confusion as the newspapermen were driven away at the beginning of the conference. His metallic features were unusually grim.

Chapter XVI

NARROW MARGINS

DOC SAVAGE had lived for a number of years a life of almost continuous peril, and the fact that he was still alive could be attributed to the amount of forethought he used. He never went into a danger, if he could avoid it, without fully preparing in advance for anything that might happen, either by accident or by the design of his opponents.

In the present situation, however, he was handicapped by circumstances. He was aboard the old steamer with only the devices which happened to be in his carry-all vest—and the vest was not loaded with a fight such as this in mind. The contents of the vest, of course, rarely remained the same for any two engagements. He changed the gadgets in the pockets to fit situations.

Doc was handicapped additionally because his physical condition was bad. He had lain unconscious in the terrific sun for the better part of three days, and that was enough to sap even his carefully cultivated strength. He needed luck to defeat Everett Everett Barr, Hoke McGee and at least a score of their men, both Lazy Y cowboys and sailors. He needed a great deal of luck.

He had some almost at once. It was bad. He encountered Sagebrush Smith and half a dozen newspaper reporters in the corridor. Sagebrush had a six-shooter in his hand, and he was telling the journalists that no man on earth could hit fifty silver dimes thrown into the air.

"Hey!" Sagebrush bawled. "There's Doc Savage!"

If there was any one on the far side of the island, they heard the cowboy's yell.

Doc Savage put on speed.

"Hey!" roared Sagebrush. "Stop or I'll shoot!"

Doc Savage did not stop. Sagebrush did not shoot. The bronze man dropped down a companionway with flashing haste, and the newspapermen began to shout; and their cries were taken up, so that the tidings throbbed through the dirty old ship.

"Doc Savage is aboard!"

The bronze man whipped toward the bow, where his men and Sally Surett were confined. The insides of the old ship were dark and unventilated, and lights had to be burned, even in the daytime.

The bronze man watched for exposed wiring, found none, and leaping, tore the wire guard from an electric bulb. He twisted out the bulb, wadded the wire guard into a cone and jammed it into the socket. Green flame and molten metal spurted, and the lights went out as a fuse blew.

Doc Savage went into the corridor where his men were confined.

"Quick, give me the keys!" he shouted.

He used an excellent imitation of Hoke McGee's unpleasant voice.

"Hurry up with those keys!" Doc snarled. "We're gonna take the prisoners out one at a time! They've gotta be taken outta there!"

Talking about taking the prisoners out, using Hoke McGee's voice, Doc kept the two guards occupied until he was upon them. One guard was taken easily. A blow of a fist dropped him. The other man jumped back.

"What's goin' on here?" he roared.

The fellow fired off his rifle, evidently hoping the flash would show what was happening. Doc Savage took hold of the rifle with one hand and twisted it aside. He then grabbed the back of the man's neck with the other hand, and his corded bronze fingers, experienced and as strong as human sinew and bone could be, did something to the man's spinal nerve centers—exerted a pressure which rendered the man helpless while still conscious. The man dropped. Doc Savage searched both guards.

They did not have the keys.

"MONK! Renny! Hit the door!" Doc Savage ordered grimly. "They're going to dynamite the ship!"

Heavy bodies crashed against the other side of the door. It was steel, old and rusted, but solid. It only grunted.

"Get back!" Doc ordered. "I'll try the rifle on the lock!"

He never got to do that. A man appeared at the other end of the corridor with a flashlight and a rifle. The light jumped against the bronze man, and the rifle crashed almost instantly. Doc reeled, went down.

"Got 'im!" the man with the rifle bellowed.

He was an optimist. His bullet had hit the bronze man in the chest, smashed the contents of two pockets in the vest, and flattened against the alloy metal mesh which underlay the vest and made it bulletproof.

Doc Savage got up. He still held the rifle of the guard, but he did not fire it. Instead, he tossed it through the grille of the brig door.

"Try to shoot your way out!" he ordered.

His voice was strained. The rifle bullet against his chest had taken his breath away, and bruised a rib or two.

Doc's hand went into his vest and got a weapon he always carried: smoke bombs. They were tiny, a little larger than marbles, and when he tossed a few down the passage, they sprouted intensely black smoke which defeated the beams of the flashlight.

The bronze man whipped toward the bow. He had to get below in the hold, stop the lighting of the fuses to the explosive. That meant reaching a hatch. And to do that, he would have to leave the superstructure, cross a short stretch of deck and drop down a hatch.

He turned a corner and came up against a six-shooter in the hand of Sagebrush Smith.

Sagebrush squinted. He lowered his gun.

"I've decided to string with you," the cowboy grunted. "There's somethin' about that Barr that smells. I don't trust no guy that Hoke McGee works for."

Doc Savage said, "Dynamite in the hold. They're going to sink the ship."

"We oughta do somethin' about it," Sagebrush Smith muttered.

He followed the bronze man. They turned right, then left, sprinted onto the open deck—and saw the forward hatch had been closed. They wrenched at it. It was fastened below. A bullet came past so close that its sound was a brittle crack. Doc Savage and Sagebrush Smith went down behind the outthrust hatch.

It was only a few yards to the cargo boom to which the plane was tethered. Two men were scrambling along this. Barr and Hoke McGee. The blonde fake Sally Surett was already aboard the plane, along with Lazy Y men and others.

Doc Savage leaped from the shelter of the hatch, ran to the boom, ran out along it. Barr turned his head, saw the bronze man. Barr squawked in fright, gave a wild leap, landed on the plane. Hoke McGee was close behind him.

Doc Savage, reaching the plane, ignored the two men. Others, who were trying to cast off the lashings which held the aircraft to the boom, were more important. He plunged into the group. One went overboard. The others closed with the bronze man in a dogfight too close, too fast, too violent, for guns to be used. One at a time, men were knocked off the plane.

Once, Doc Savage nearly went over the side, stayed aboard only because he struck with one foot and drove it through the thin sheet-metal of a wing of the plane. A moment later, the last Lazy Y man went into the water.

Everett Everett Barr evidently had no gun, and Hoke McGee must have emptied his, because they did not shoot. Instead, they turned wildly, scrambled onto the boom and clawed back for the deck of the steamer.

Sagebrush Smith stood at the head of the boom and pointed his six-gun at the two men.

"Get yer hands up, dang you!" he ordered.

Hoke McGee and Everett Everett Barr were too terrified to react normally to the threat. They seemed unaware of the gun—or they might have still thought that Sagebrush Smith did not know they were enemies. They reached the deck, and raced wildly for a companionway.

"Don't light the fuse!" Barr screamed. *"Don't light the fuse!"*

At that point, Doc Savage's men appeared on deck with Sally Surett.

CONFUSION was everywhere on the steamer. The newspapermen—most of whom had been pounding out stories of the latest development on their typewriters—charged out on deck and bellowed questions at every one. Below decks, men were shouting and shooting, staging the fake break by Doc Savage's aids which was to precede the blast. They still did not know that the break had turned into a genuine one.

Doc Savage, having cleared the plane, lifted his voice.

"Get aboard the plane!" he shouted. "Get boats over the side! Leave the steamer!"

His remarkable voice had a crashing volume and a penetrating vibrancy that echoed throughout the ship.

"They're setting off an explosion in the hold!" Doc explained.

The news was a little too astounding for instant acceptance. Newspaper reporters lined the rail, or hid behind ventilators, and demanded to know what was going on.

Doc Savage's five assistants scrambled out on the cargo boom, helping Sally Surett, and dropped aboard. Sagebrush Smith followed.

"Get off the steamer!" Doc shouted. "There is going to be an explosion."

A rifle smacked once, viciously, from the wheelhouse window. Renny grunted loudly, took hold of his leg, and nearly went overboard. Monk grabbed him. They got into the cabin of the plane.

The rifle whacked again, and the bullet bored into the plane, narrowly missing Sally Surett.

Sagebrush Smith said, "I'll fix that jasper!"

He aimed carefully with his six-gun, fired. "Daggone!" he said.

He fired again.

"The guy is shootin' from an openin' about an inch wide," he muttered.

He shot once more.

"Ah!" he said. "That's sure a small target!"

Doc Savage reached for the cowboy's gun.

"Wait a minute!" Sagebrush Smith said. "This takes *shootin'!*"

The bronze man grasped the six-shooter, and an astonished Sagebrush Smith, who had a good grip on the gun, found the weapon removed from his fingers as though he hadn't wanted to hold to it at all.

Doc lifted the six-gun; there was no perceptible interval of aim; the gun whacked. The menacing rifle muzzle jumped back out of sight.

Sagebrush Smith looked foolish.

The steamer jumped to pieces in the middle. The funnel went up first, not straight up, but slanting off toward the sun. Then the superstructure lifted, parting in the center, splitting, windows and portholes flying out from the main bulk, followed by smaller timbers.

A whole man seemed to fly up and out farther than anything else. His limbs moved like the legs of an ant while he was in the air, and he seemed suspended for such a long time that it appeared possible his fall into the sea would not injure him; but while he was still fifty feet above the water, falling débris overtook and mangled him.

After the superstructure jumped a few feet into the air, the sides of the ship laid over in the water. One of the sides laid on the plane, but did it so gently, that the plane was only pushed a little bit beneath the surface. The plane bobbed up like a cork as soon as the wreckage slid off into the water with gurgling sounds.

Doc Savage and his men were very busy for the next hour, bringing in survivors, and busy for the next two days caring for the injured. By that time, U. S. Coast Guard planes and other aircraft had arrived, and a Coast Guard cutter put in an appearance.

They listened to the bronze man's story of what had happened, a version that was verified by Everett Everett Barr's wife, whose spirit had broken. She had remained aboard the plane, and had escaped the blast.

"What about Everett Everett Barr?" was the immediate question.

Sagebrush Smith answered that.

"We found 'im," Sagebrush said.

"How is he?"

"He's dead enough," Sagebrush said, "so that everybody oughta be satisfied."

EVERYBODY was fairly well satisfied, even the gullibles who had put up nearly three hundred thousand dollars for Everett Everett Barr to use in finding Captain Scuttle's treasure. Barr's widow got them most of their money back. Of course, the newspapers weren't satisfied. They had made clowns out of themselves.

Hoke McGee wasn't satisfied, either. At first, he had been very glad to be alive, but it was beginning to seem very much as if the authorities were going to remedy that via the electric chair.

Sally Surett, the genuine one, was very well satisfied. She was a quiet little girl with a very sweet disposition and all the men promptly fell in love with her, including Monk, Ham and Sagebrush Smith. The young lady seemed to prefer Sagebrush Smith.

"She shows good judgment," big-fisted Renny told Monk and Ham.

Which was nearly the cause of his having to fight both Monk and Ham, who were still quarreling with Sagebrush when they weren't squabbling with each other.

"You two mugs," Renny told them, "have been so busy with your quarreling that you haven't had time to make love. No wonder the cowboy got the girl."

Doc Savage, using deep-water diving equipment which had been sent from New York by air express, and brought down by a chartered plane, descended to the sunken steamer. The water was well over two hundred feet deep. He brought up old Meander Surett's device.

"The strange thing," he told Sally Surett, "is that your father's apparatus utilized a theory along which science has done almost no development. It is possible that, had he lived, and had he been brought out of the mentally depressing surroundings of Death Valley, he might actually have made the thing work. I am going to ask the newspapers to make that clear."

"They're saying," the girl said gently, "that my father was a crazy inventor."

"I know. And they are wrong."

The young woman nodded gratefully. It was a matter of no importance to the world, now, whether or not her father had been mad; but to her it meant a great deal, and she was grateful to the bronze man for perceiving that and doing something about it. She explained as much to Sagebrush Smith later.

Sagebrush Smith approached Doc Savage. He was embarrassed.

"Daggone," he said, "I wonder if you'd do me a favor?"

"What?"

The gangling cowboy began scooping silver dimes from his pockets to his hat.

"I've been tradin' everybody outta their dimes," he said. "I finally got fifty here. I want you and me to go off somewhere on the island where that dingbusted Monk and Ham won't be around to razz me, and I wanta see you hit fifty dimes with fifty shots from a revolver."

"Is it important to you?" Doc asked.

"Kinda. You see—ah—well, I'm thinkin' of makin' a change in myself."

Doc and the cowboy went to a secluded spot. Sagebrush Smith threw up dimes. Doc Savage stood beside him and fired. The bronze man hit forty-nine of the dimes.

Sagebrush Smith put the fiftieth dime back in his pocket.

"I've got a hunch I'd feel better if you didn't hit all fifty," he explained sheepishly. "This fifty-dimes-with-fifty-shots business has been a kind of important thing with me for years."

The cowboy rubbed his jaw.

"It's been an ambition of mine to see you do that," he said.

He took off his hat, scowled at it, put it back on and scratched the back of his neck.

"Ain't that a hell of an ambition for a grown man to have?" he demanded disgustedly. "I'm just a dang saddle bum! Just a shiftin' cow waddy with no gumption and no ambition but to sling a six-gun. Ah—bugs!"

Doc Savage studied Sagebrush Smith, and knew he was examining a young man who had wasted a good part of his life on trivialities, only to suddenly awaken and find himself in love with a swell girl whom he was unable to support.

"I have been wondering," the bronze man said, "if you would care to establish and manage a dude ranch and winter resort in the mountains back East. Of course, a married man would be preferable, but——"

"I can fix that!" Sagebrush grinned.

The cowboy went gravely to the edge of the cliff where the shooting had been done. With some solemnity, he removed his six-shooter from his trousers waistband, drew back and hurled it as far out into the sea as he could lob it.

"That," Sagebrush Smith said, "is what I should 'a' done as soon as I was big enough to throw it."